LOOKING AFTER YOUR
DINGHY

Terry Smith

Illustrator
Helen Downton

Designer
Anthony Lawrence

Pelham Books London

Looking After Your Dinghy was
conceived and edited by Imogen Bright,
21 Weedon Lane, Amersham, Bucks.

Designer Anthony Lawrence
Illustrator Helen Downton

First published in Great Britain by
Pelham Books Ltd., 44 Bedford Square,
London WC1B 3DU, 1983

British Library Cataloguing in Publication Data

Smith, Terry, *19__*
    Looking after your dinghy.
    1. Sailboats — Maintenance and repairs
    I. Title
    623.8'223   VM351

ISBN 0 7207 1431 1 Paperback
ISBN 0 7207 1461 3 Hardback

Printed and Bound in Great Britain by Hollen
Street Press Ltd., Slough

CONTENTS

THE BOAT AND ITS EQUIPMENT

If you are new to boats or sailing, you may not be acquainted with all the sailing terms or with the names of the different parts of a boat and its equipment. The illustrations here will help to make you familiar with the names you will encounter later in the book, and will also help you to talk the language to other sailors.

1. Mainsail
2. Mainsheet
3. Batten Pocket
4. Jib (Foresail)
5. Spinnaker
6. Spinnaker Chute
7. Stemhead
8. Chainplate
9. Rowlock
10. Gunwale
11. Coaming
12. Rubbing Bead
13. Transom
14. Transom Flap
15. Rudder
16. Rudder Stock
17. Tiller
18. Tiller Extension
19. Mast Step
20. Bulkhead
21. Buoyancy Bag
22. Buoyancy Tank
23. Kicking Strap
24. Centrecase
25. Centreboard
26. Thwart
27. Traveller
28. Self-Bailer
29. Toe Strap
30. Hog
31. Muscle Box
32. Block
33. Fairlead
34. Cleat
35. Track
36. Mast = Spar
37. Boom = Spar
38. Hounds
39. Sheave
40. Shroud = Standing Rigging
41. Trapeze = Standing Rigging
42. Forestay = Standing Rigging
43. Halliard = Running Rigging
44. Spinnaker Pole
45. Hook Up Rack
46. Gooseneck
47. Tack Pin
48. Clew Outhaul
49. Lug
50. Highfield Lever
51. Burgee
52. Keel
53. Keel Band
54. Chine
55. Bilge Rubber
56. Skeg

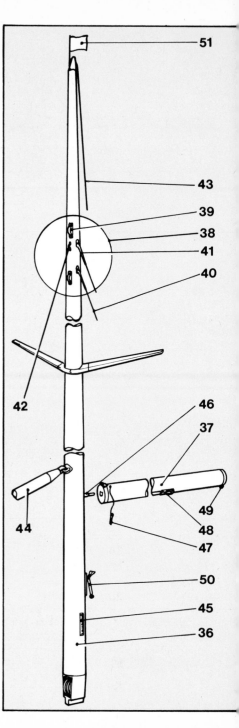

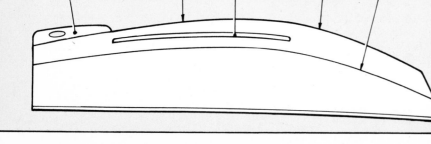

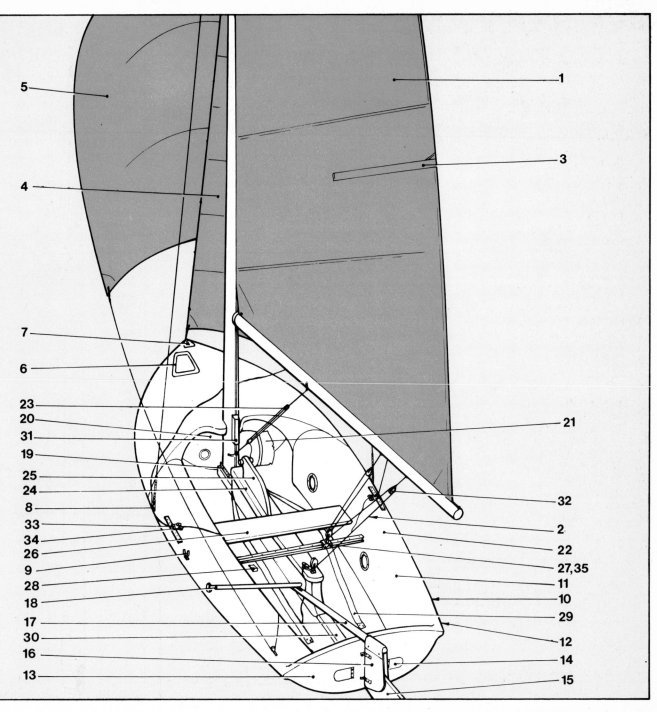

HOW TO CHOOSE

Never buy a boat on impulse. Ask yourself a few questions. Will you be racing or cruising? Where will you keep the boat? Do you wish to join a sailing club? Which type or class of dinghy would suit you best?

General Hints A visit to some sailing clubs where you could talk to owners of different dinghies and perhaps have a trial sail would help you to decide. If possible, choose a boat with an active Class Association. A boat without an Association, or one peculiar to one club will have limited resale value.

If you require the boat for cruising, consider the conditions you are likely to meet. Is there a slipway, or will the boat be left on moorings? If the boat is to be used in conjunction with a touring caravan, it must be light enough to put on top of the car. How many members of the family do you expect to take with you at a time? If you wish to go rowing or to use an outboard engine, check that the boat is suitable. If you require a performance dinghy to double as a yacht tender, this will restrict the size of boat you choose.

Obtain full insurance cover befor you take the boat out for a sail, or whil you are still building. You shoul obtain third party cover in case yo cause damage to another boat. Chec that the policy covers situations suc as slipping the boat into the water an trailing. The total should cover th price you paid for the boat, the fittings sails and any repairs that have to b done. Remember that if you insure five year old boat and it is damage beyond repair, you can only expect five year old boat to replace it.

If you are buying your first boat remember also to budget for extr items such as sails, trolleys, covers lifejackets and special clothing.

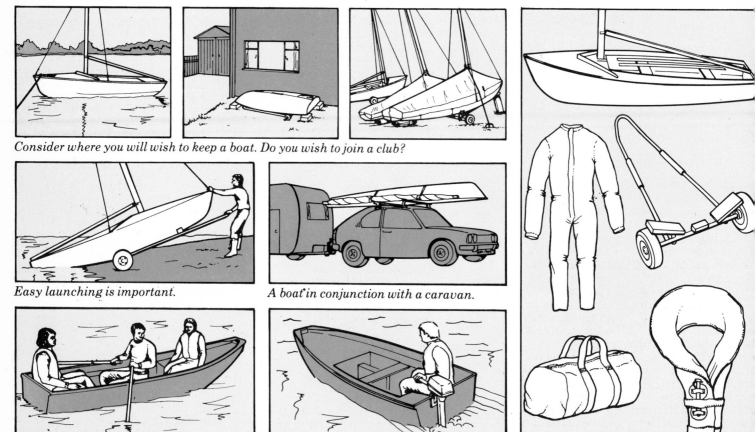

Consider where you will wish to keep a boat. Do you wish to join a club?

Easy launching is important.

A boat in conjunction with a caravan.

Will you wish to take the family rowing?

Will you want to use an outboard motor?

Remember to budget for all the extras.

New Boat You can either buy a boat complete from a builder, a boat in kit form or one in various stages of construction. Home completion means considerable savings in cost, and personal touches which are uneconomical for the professional builder to include can be added.

Before deciding to build a boat yourself, consider such points as whether you have adequate space to do the job, whether you possess the necessary skills (some boats are more difficult to build than others) and whether you can borrow or hire the specialist tools required.

Building your own boat saves money, but you need space, special tools and skills.

During construction obtain a copy of the measurement rules from the Class Association, and keep within the tolerances allowed. Check also what alternatives can be incorporated.

If you wish to buy a completed boat, get several quotations and check on the reputation of the different builders. Before buying through an agent, compare the prices of several agencies. Obtain a full inventory of what is included in the price, but do not rush into buying a lot of extras. Seek advice on these, and if in doubt leave them out. Most additional items can be fitted at a later date, with the exception of spinnaker chutes and self-bailers

which are often easier to fit in the workshop.

It is worth visiting the factory or boatyard in order to check on the quality of the materials being used. Some builders skimp on the gel coat or use inferior timber. Ask the builder what alternative finishes he has to offer, and choose one suited to your needs (*see* **Coatings and Finishes**).

Before accepting the boat, make sure that it will measure according to

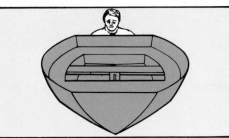

Sight along the bulkheads to check for twists in the hull.

the rules of the Class Association, and that their recommendations are followed. Look out for bad workmanship, particularly bad glue joints (*see* **Have you a Problem?**), which could cause serious problems early in the life of the boat. Make a thorough check as soon as possible. If you have any subsequent complaints write to the supplier and the builder, although it will be the builder who will be most anxious to put matters right.

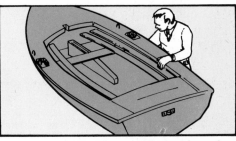

Check a new boat thoroughly inside and out for bad workmanship.

Before accepting the boat, make sure that it weighs and measures correctly according to the Class Association rules.

SECONDHAND

You will find advertisements for secondhand boats in the local press and yachting magazines or on the notice boards of local sailing clubs. A visit to a club is a good way of finding out about boats for sale.

These are the basic do's and don'ts when buying a boat secondhand:

1. Do not choose a boat because of price or colour.
2. Find out as much as possible about the boat advertized. Contact the Class Association or the builder quoting the sail number to check the date of building or purchase. Do not accept that a boat is professionally built without proof.
3. Research into the class of dinghy thoroughly, as some classes (e.g. the Enterprise) have had design changes to correct a source of weakness. Knowledge of these changes will help you to assess the true value of the boat.

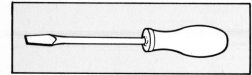
Screwdriver and knife to inspect a boat.

4. Avoid home-designed, non-class boats. The materials, rig and buoyancy can be inadequate.
5. Be wary of boats that have been raced strenuously, and are being sold after a season or two.
6. If the price does not include extras like sails, trolley and trailer, try to persuade the vendor to let you have these for an inclusive price. This is far the cheapest way when you are buying your first boat.
7. If the boat needs repairing, obtain an estimate for the work so that you can check that the asking price for the boat is fair.
8. Insist that a Class boat has a measurement certificate.
9. Once you have decided on a boat ask the vendor what system has been used to finish the hull and keep a record for when you repaint. Application of finishes which are not compatible can be expensive.

Take someone who knows about boats with you to make the inspection. Take a screwdriver and a sharp knife so that you can make the proper checks. Listen, preferably with a witness, to what the vendor says about the boat, and keep a copy of the advertisement in case the boat does not meet the specification.

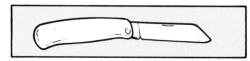

The most common faults to look for are rot in timber, crazing in the gel coat on GRP boats and leaky buoyancy. You can find detailed information on the points listed here by referring to the index.

Further checks to carry out are:

1. Use the knife to test timber for decay. Scrape off any suspect paint.

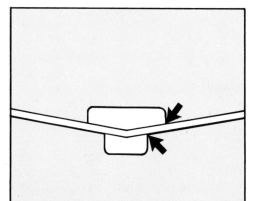
Check hog and keel for rot.

Test for soft wood.

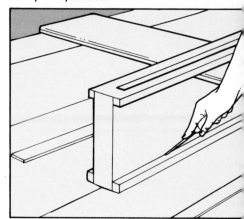
Test glue joins.

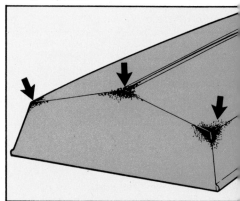
Look out for black stains.

. Beware of a newly painted hull, as
his could be a cover up.
. Beware of big repairs, especially
here a large quantity of fibreglass
ller has been used. Prod the repair
ith your knife.
. Turn the boat upside down, and look
long the hull at different angles.

Irregular bumps or hollows in the
normal curving lines will suggest a
repair or bad construction.
5. Inspect the keel band and the bottom
panels. If necessary check the
condition of the fixing points by
removing the screws.
6. Extend the centreboard and check

that it is true with the boat.
7. With the boat the right way up look
at each bulkhead and gunwale line in
relation to the transom. This will show
if the boat has a twist in the hull.
8. Check the quality of the fittings and
spars. The vendor may have kept his
best fittings for his new boat.

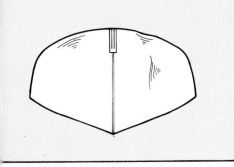

Beware of repairs with lots of filler.

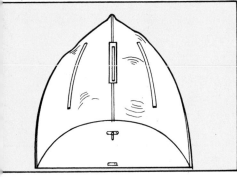

Look for bumps and hollows.

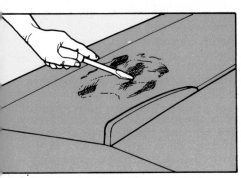

Look for stress cracks on GRP.

Remove keel band screw.

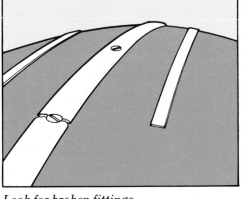

Look for broken fittings.

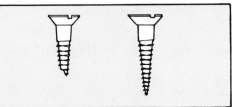

Check all fastenings.

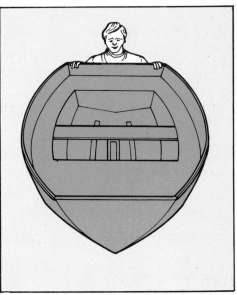

Is the centreboard true with the boat?

Is there a twist in the hull?

IS THE BOAT READY TO GO?

Before taking the boat for a sail, rig it completely to check that everything works. Make sure you know how it all fits together.

Make sure that the rudder pivots easily on the transom fittings. If the fittings are out of true, this could cause a breakage. Does the centreboard move up and down easily in the case, and will it stay in various positions? If the pivot bolt is loose, it could induce leaks, but do not over-tighten.

Replace any frayed ropes or shock cord, and check the wire rigging for broken strands or bad discoloration. Cover with strong tape any points in the rigging that could catch hands or clothing.

The basic equipment you will need for your boat is: a bucket and sponge for washing down; a bailer; a paddle; an anchor if you intend to sail offshore; a burgee or racing flag.

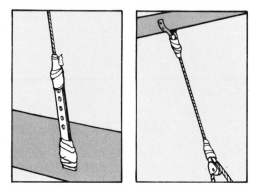

Tape any catching points.

Make sure that the boat is tidy. The floor should be clear of obstacles, and nothing should be allowed to roll around. Tie the paddle and the bailer to the boat. Additional straps sewn onto the buoyancy bag webbing and fastened with Velcro are safer for the paddle or jib stick than poking them between the buoyancy bags and the straps. If your Class rules allow, you can screw an aluminium strip to the boom for the spinnaker pole. Fit pockets for the halliards to the deck beam or under the deck. One way of storing spare and small articles is to fit a plastic container into the inspection hatch ring of the buoyancy chambers. Various sizes of plastic tube are useful for slotting things into or as straps. Nylon clips are simple and safe provided they are out of the way.

Basic boat equipment.

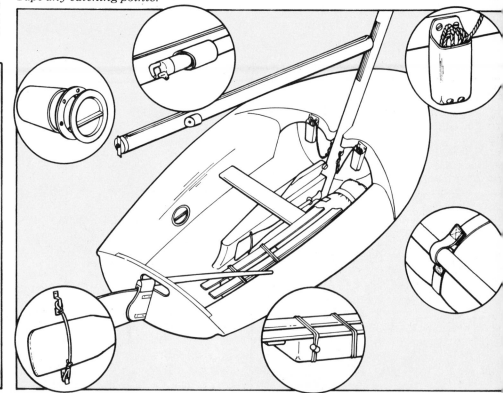

Make sure that the boat is tidy, and tie up anything that can roll around.

As soon as you slip the boat into the water look carefully for leakages. Once you have begun sailing it will be difficult to tell where the water is coming from.

During the first few outings get to know the boat intimately and carry out as many manoeuvres as possible. Work everything that is supposed to work. Change places with the crew so that you can see things from another angle. If the rudder or centreboard vibrate or hum, they require some work (*see* **Centreboard and Rudder**). Check the tiller extension. If it is loose, the universal joint needs attention or replacing. If it is slippery to hold, fix a pad to provide a firm grip.

Avoid all kinds of chafing.

Does the spinnaker system work well for you, or can you improve it? Consider other possible systems and look at other boats. Does the kicking strap suit you? What is the most effective way to lead the controls and halliards?

Make sure that the boat is comfortable. Are there any sharp edges? Do the cockpit coamings and seats require rounding off? Flattening the rubbing beads helps for leaning out, and also clears the water away from the deck join. Are there any toe straps? Are they correctly positioned? There should be no slippery surfaces. If necessary apply a non-slip material to the floor, and to the gunwale of a trapeze boat.

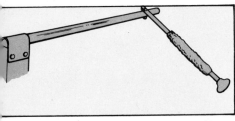

Tiller extensions should be easy to hold.

Check that the fittings and controls are doing their job efficiently. Check that the control lines are readily accessible. Check that the lines are not being chafed by the blocks or leads entering them at the wrong angle.

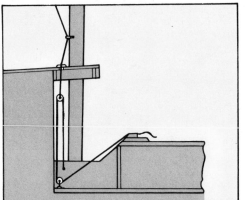

A good way to lead control lines.

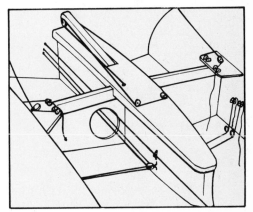

Is it better to lead controls lines aft?

Bush panels to avoid chafing.

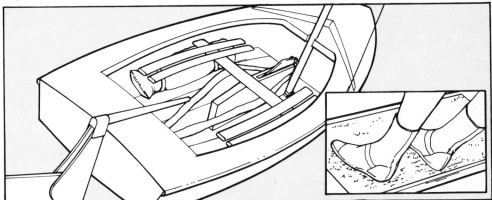

Is the boat comfortable to sit in? On a trapeze boat use non-slip material (inset).

EQUIPMENT

Whether you are racing or cruising, you will always need a good set of tools and to carry spare fittings with you. If you cannot deal with problems and emergencies fast and efficiently, the result will be lost sailing time. You should also assemble a First Aid box (*see* Hull Care and Maintenance).

Tools
Sailing knife, the most basic and essential tool
Shackle tool, some come with a screwdriver and spanner
Pliers
Spanners, avoid adjustable spanners, as they seize up when wet.
Buy the open ended type to suit the nuts on your boat
Screwdrivers, various sizes
Claw hammer
Pin hammer
Junior hacksaw and spare blades
Drill and two or three different size bits
Strong adhesive tape
Scissors
Sail needles and different size threads
Kit containing eyelets and rings and tool for repairing covers
Matches and heat shrinks
Nylon fishing line and weight for halliards
Wax polish spray/petroleum jelly to ease stiff fittings
Notebook and pencils
Tape measure
File
Chisel
Bradawl
Splicing tool, a 6″ (15 cm) oval nail with the point filed off will do
Toothbrush

Spares
Shackles and rigging links
Stainless steel self-tapping screws, various sizes
Brass or stainless steel machine screws $\frac{3}{16}$″ and $\frac{1}{4}$″ (5 mm and 6 mm) diameter and 2″ (50 mm) long, can be cut to length
Nuts to suit pivot bolts
Cleats
Rope, various lengths and sizes
Shock cord
Halliards and kicking strap
Cork or rubber bungs
Gooseneck fittings
Transom fittings
Cotter pin for the tiller
Battens
Telltales
Burgee/racing flag

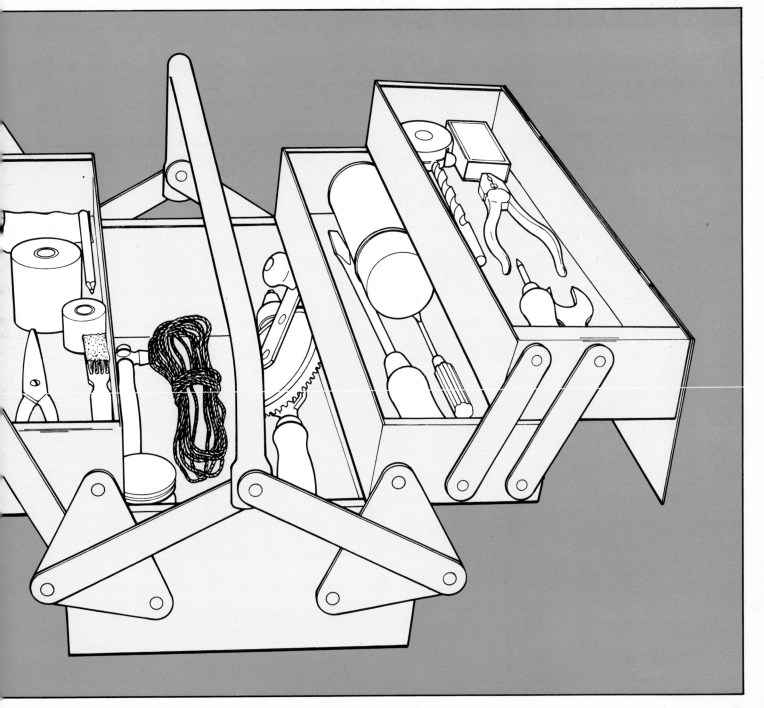

IN THE DINGHY PARK

Whenever the boat is stored outside it is vital to avoid damp. Ventilation is very important, but almost impossible if the boat is covered up. If you are unable to visit your boat very often, ask a friend to open it up on a fine day to allow ventilation. This is also a useful security point.

Covers (see **Covers**) are never completely watertight, and some water is bound to enter the boat. Water will always collect in the centre of the boat, particularly around the centrecase. If it persistently collects in one place, it could cause damage. The boat should therefore always be left so that it drains automatically. Most boats will drain if positioned with the bows up and the transom down. Boats which do not have a direct passage to the stern should be left so that water drains through the opened self-bailer.

Take down the burgee, and wash down the boat thoroughly (see **Hull Care and Maintenance**). Remove the inspection covers to the buoyancy tanks. Leave the transom flaps open to allow air flow. Place the bucket so that it catches the drips from the mast. Take a small piece of rope (natural fibre if possible), and thread both ends through the drain holes in the transom so that the middle of the rope dangles outside. This creates a capillary action to remove the last drops of water from the back of the boat.

Remove all sails and lifejackets. Otherwise they can encourage damp, and also other people to sail your boat.

Coil the sheets loosely and drape them over the side seats or thwart. Tightly coiled ropes can trap water. Do not leave the rudder on the floor where it can restrict the flow of water.

Attach the ends of the halliards to the bow plate and cleat them, tight but not tensioned. If you shackle them to the mast, tie the halliards out to the shrouds so that they do not chafe against the mast and make an irritating noise.

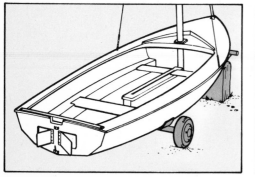

Leave the boat to drain automatically.

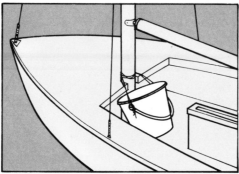

Place the bucket to catch mast drips.

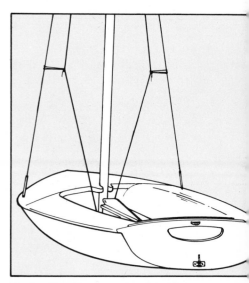

Tie halliards out to the shrouds.

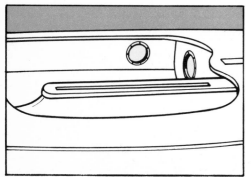

Remove inspection covers and bungs.

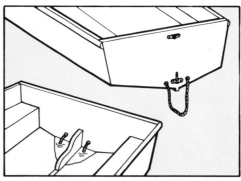

Thread some rope to help drainage.

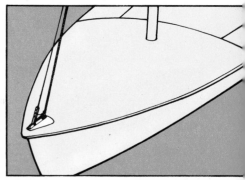

. . . Or cleat halliards to bowplate.

You must avoid large pockets of water forming in the cover. If a flat cover or a travelling cover is used, form a ridge with a length of timber down the centre of the boat to shed water. If you use a boom-up cover, the boom should sit on the transom resting on a piece of wood. If the boom is too short, make an extension from a plastic drainpipe. Secure the boom to the mast with a length of string or shock cord after fitting it onto the gooseneck. Do not use the kicking strap, as the tension will cause a permanent bend in the boom.

Never allow the boat to be in contact with the ground or damp surfaces. It must be correctly supported with the main weight taken on the keel, bilge keels or chines. Rest the transom on a cradle or tyre, well off the ground. To prevent the boat being blown over, rope it down to stakes on either side. Suggest that your neighbours do the same, as their boats could cause more damage to your boat than to their own.

If you leave your boat on a road trailer, immobilize it by removing the hitch. Otherwise anyone could drive the boat away.

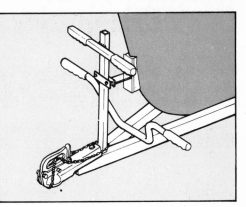

Trailer hitch immobilized for security.

Travelling cover with length of timber.

Hints for using a boom-up cover.

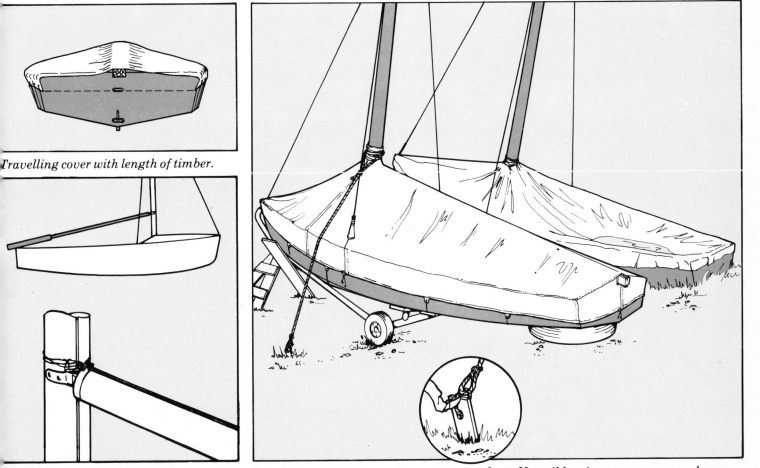

The right and the wrong way to store your boat. Note ribbon in case grass grows long.

COVERS

Dinghies kept outside need the protection of a cover. GRP boats need protection from ultra violet light, dust and leaves. While the boat is stored your main concern is to prevent water from collecting on the cover or leaking into the boat through the openings.

There are three types of cover available.

The travelling cover is completely flat and is the only cover that does not leak, since it has no openings at all. Disadvantage: you have to take down the mast each time.

The flat cover has openings for the mast and shrouds. Not recommended, since ventilation is bad and water gets trapped.

The boom-up cover is the most suitable type. It sheds water easily, and allows ventilation. However, the mast and shroud openings leak.

Covers are also available in various materials. The principal types are as follows:

Unsupported PVC is the cheapest material, but in order to achieve the necessary strength, it is thick and heavy. As the material cannot be sewn, mast and shroud openings are poor.

PVC on nylon or woven base is strong and light, and can be well tailored to fit boats. Choose a cover with welded rather than sewn seams, which leak. PVC can be affected by ultra violet light and becomes brittle. To prevent it resting on the surface of the boat fix extra ties or lay shock cord over the boom and hook under the rubbing beads.

Cotton duck canvas is the most expensive material, but ideal for dinghy covers, as it can be sewn and is flexible. A cloth weight of 12 oz before proofing is recommended. When making up make allowances for the fact that canvas shrinks.

Always roll up the cover before going sailing. Do not fold or leave on the ground. If any water has collected on the cover, the scum can cause

damage, so wash it off. After sailing you should tie the collar around the mast and the shroud openings first. These are the principal sources of leaks, so take care to fasten well. Close the foredeck join and tension the under ties last. Keep the cover taut, but no

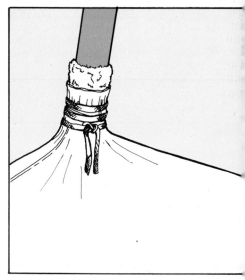

Poor mast and shroud openings.

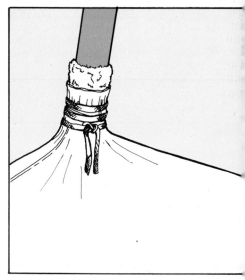

Wrap an old towel around the mast.

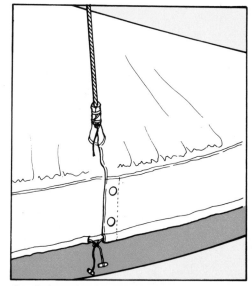

Good shroud ties will prevent leaks.

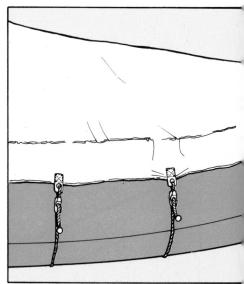

Good underties taut against the wind.

over-stretched. A loose cover will flap and wear quickly.

In order to reduce leaks around the mast collar wrap an old towel around the mast, letting it stick out of the top of the collar. A ½″ (12 mm) wide soft webbing makes a more efficient tie around the collar than rope, and causes less wear to the cover material. If any fittings protrude into the cover, place a pad or sponge (wrapped in polythene so that it does not absorb water) over the fitting, or reinforce the cover at this point. A small cord sewn onto the back edge of the cover and tied to the transom pintle will prevent the cover sagging inside the transom.

The mast and shroud collars, the eyelets or securing points for the ties and the ropes themselves should be watched for wear. Corners require attention and should be reinforced if necessary. Attend to tears or cracks immediately. Replace worn or broken lashings. Do not use rope less than ½″ circ. (4 mm in diameter). Thinner cords cut into the hull.

For tears glue a patch onto the outside of the cover, using the same or similar material. Sew around the tear and through the patch, and then sew around the edge of the patch onto the cover. With canvas use waxed thread. PVC covers will leak around the seams, so stick adhesive tape over stitching. If an eyelet pulls out, reinforce the area with canvas or webbing, and fix the new eyelet into this.

At the end of each season scrub canvas with fresh water. Dry thoroughly, and brush on a wax emulsion to preserve and waterproof it. PVC covers should be washed with warm soapy water, rinsed and dried. Roll up covers, and store away from direct sunlight.

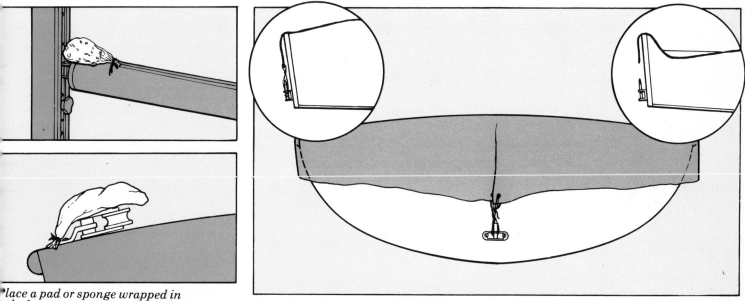

Place a pad or sponge wrapped in polythene over any protruding fittings.

A small cord sewn to cover and tied to transom fitting.

Reinforce corners if necessary.   *Mend any tears using a patch.*   *Reinforce eyelet fixing points; using kit to fit new eyelet.*

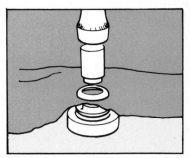

WINTER STORAGE

Wherever you decide to keep your boat for the winter, it is essential to keep it dry and well ventilated. Frequent checks during the hibernation period could spotlight trouble before it is too late.

Before leaving the boat for the winter check the hull and equipment thoroughly. Make one list of the jobs to be done, so that you allow time before the start of the season, and a second list of what you need to buy to carry out these jobs.

If you need professional help on the boat, the end of the year is the best time to contact boatbuilders. If you need to send away spars or sails, tie a label on each item with your name and address, the article, the class and number of dinghy (Mainsail for Fireball no. —), together with full details of the damage or alteration.

Make lists. Label items to be sent away.

Strip the boat of all possible gear which could retain water - ropes, webbing, etc. Remove the buoyancy bags, inspection covers and all drainage plugs. Wash the boat thoroughly and swill out the buoyancy tanks if accessible. Remove excess water with a leather. Wash all the fittings, especially the ropes. Dry out thoroughly. If you store the boat and the gear in different places, make a list of all the equipment.

Wrap the centreboard and rudder in an old curtain or sheet, and store them completely flat in a dry place. Weight them down to prevent warping, and store them away from sunlight or heat (including central heating pipes under the floorboards). Put a timber packing in the centrecase slot to prevent warping.

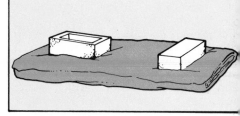
Weight down centreboard and rudder.

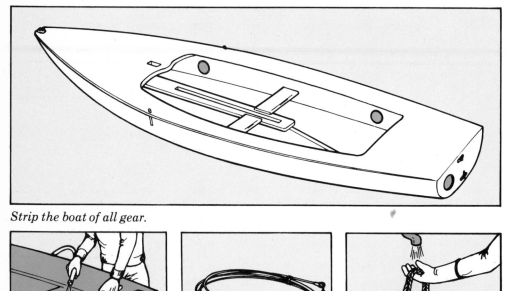
Strip the boat of all gear.

Wash the boat thoroughly. Coil wires. Wash ropes and fittings.

Put timber packing in the centrecase.

Wash the spars thoroughly in soapy water to remove all traces of salt or dirt. Remove all loose fittings, especially the standing rigging. Remove the halliards, but leave string threaded in their place. Before storing varnish a wooden mast or wax polish a metal mast. Provided they are kept straight, spars can be kept outside, but they must not be in contact with the damp ground. If storing horizontal, spars must be supported every 45″ to 55″ (1¼ to 1½ metres) and kept in a straight line so as not to cause a bow.

Masts are a problem to store, due to their size. These are a few storage suggestions:

Under the eaves of the house.
Tied to a drainpipe.
Hung on a fence.
Up a stair well or up the stairs.
On a garage roof.
In a garage roof.
On the boat, forming a ridge for the cover.

In each case keep the luff groove at the bottom, and cover the top of the halliard sheaves so that damp and dirt cannot get in.

Wash sails and sail bags, and dry thoroughly. Do not store with other equipment on top of them.

If you leave your boat out for the winter, take extra care to ensure that the cover is secure and will not become loose or ill-fitting in the wind. If you have an ill-fitting cover, turn the boat upside down and drape the cover over. Make sure that the covering extends below the gunwale so that water cannot collect on the rubbing beads. Look out for water splashing up from the ground. Together with condensation this tends to collect on the underside of decks or inner gunwales, thus causing damage.

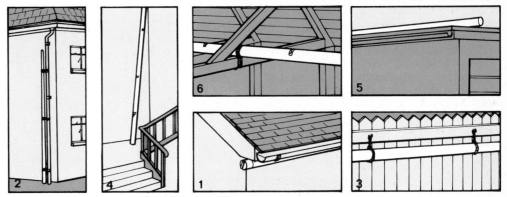

Masts are a problem to store. Choose what is most practical for you.

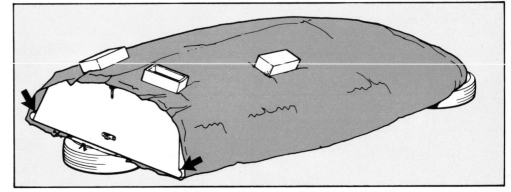

Do not leave gaps for water to collect, and tie cover tight around the boat.

Different ways of supporting a spar kept outside for the winter. Keep in a straight line, well off the damp ground.

INDOOR STORAGE

Choose a weatherproof building with adequate ventilation whenever possible. Drape a dustsheet over the boat to keep it clean. The boat must always be supported properly on its fittings. There must be no undue stress on the hull panels or deck, and the bulk of the weight should be borne on the framed areas, keel or gunwales.

Here are some suggestions:
Roof Storage Most dinghies are under 30″ (75 cm) at the deepest point, and can be stored in the roof of garages or carports. What system you use will depend on the shape of the roof. Check that the roof beams are strong enough to bear the weight of a boat.

Store the boat upside down on timbers or struts suspended from the roof structure. Hang the struts so that they will support the boat at least 24″ (60 cm) from each end. Attach the struts to the roof beams with strong ropes or supports which will enable them to be swung out of the way while

positioning the boat, and then swung back to hold it. A heavy boat may require a simple system of pulleys and ropes to haul it up into the roof. If each strut is hauled up independently, lift them a little at a time so that the boat is not suspended at a bad angle at any point.

Whichever way up the boat is kept the use of the struts is recommended. If slings or ropes are used on their own they can distort the hull. Build a narrow platform between the two struts, either under the boat or at the side, to hold the sails, covers, trolley etc. An old ladder could possibly be used as a shelf.

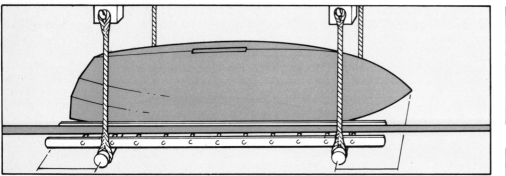
Place a strut 24″ (60 cm) from each end of the boat. Use a ladder as shelf for gear.

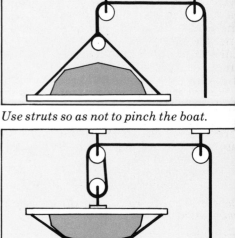
Use struts so as not to pinch the boat.

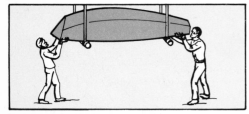
Lifting a boat into the roof.

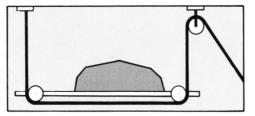
Simple pulley system.

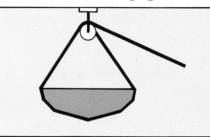
Use struts to avoid damaging the boat.

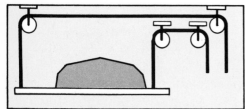
Raise boat evenly a little at a time.

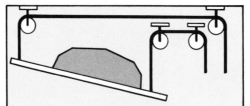

Pinching a boat.

Barn Storage If you can find a building with a high ceiling, a boat can be stored sitting on its transom. Remove the transom fittings and place padding under the boat, and place strips of wood under the chine and gunwale. Lean the boat against the wall and tie it up to prevent it slipping.

Wall Storage If the boat is framed or very rigid across the top, it can be stored against a wall, resting on the gunwale. It must be supported in three or four places, so that the strain is distributed and the hull is unable to rock. Pad the top gunwale well against chafing on the wall.

Trestles or Trailer Turn the boat upside down or cover it to stop the dirt. Check the soundness of the trestles.

Multiple Storage With care boats can be stored on top of each other. Always check that the supports are adequate and use plenty of padding between the hulls. Make sure that the keel band of one boat does not cut into the decks of the other.

When storing boats face to face, they will fit more securely if the transom of the top boat lies on the foredeck of the bottom one, and is supported by a frame or the gunwales.

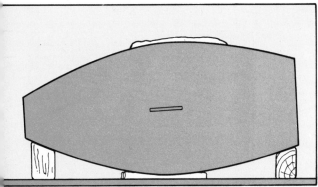

Boats can be stored sitting on the transom, using wood under chine and gunwale.

Boat stored resting on the gunwale. Pad well.

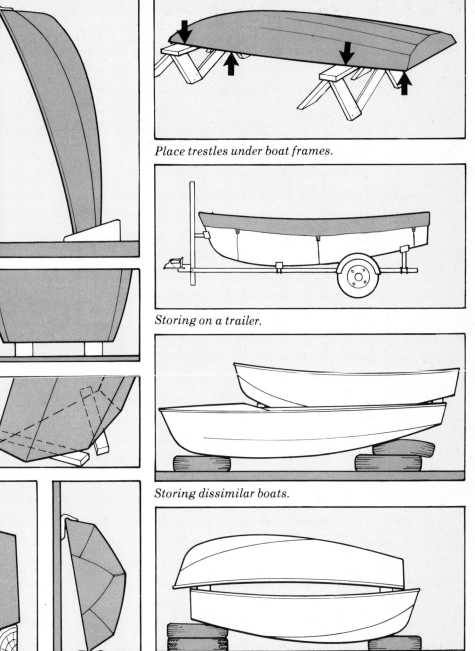

Place trestles under boat frames.

Storing on a trailer.

Storing dissimilar boats.

Storing two similar boats.

ROUTINE CHECKS

Check over your boat after each sail. Learn to cast a critical eye. This way you will pick up any problems before they become serious.

Wash the boat thoroughly both inside and out. If sailed in salt water, hose it down with fresh water, as dried salt water forms a solution of concentrated sodium chloride when added to dew. Wash off the scum around the waterline. Sponge out the sediment from the bottom of the boat, as grit will cause a scouring action next time the boat is used. Clear away any mud, leaves or weed which could clog the runnels. If the runnels are inadequate, drill or chisel them out to make them larger, but make sure that you are not infringing your Class rules. Sponge out excess water and allow to dry before covering the boat, and make sure that all water can drain away easily.

Wash sand and grit from the sheets and control lines to prevent them from becoming hard and worn. Salt, sand and grit also work their way into the moving parts of blocks, slides and bailers. Rinse these with fresh water, and sluice around the buoyancy bags and webbing straps.

When you have cleaned the boat, carry out the following checks. For detailed information on what to look for and dealing with problems, refer to the relevant page of this book with the help of the index.

1. Remove the drain plugs and hatches from the buoyancy chambers. Sponge out any trapped water, and poke a stick through drain holes to check for obstructions.
2. Look around the centrecase for cracking of the paint or varnish, which could indicate flexing of the structure.
3. Check the tightness of the centreboard bolt. If it is loose, it could induce leaks, but if you over-tighten it you could distort the centrecase.
4. The thwart(s) should be secure and holding the centrecase rigid. A glance around the glue join of the case wi[ll] pick up first signs of trouble.
5. Check the fittings (*see* **Fittings**).
6. Look at the chainplates and rudde[r] fittings for crazing in the paint or ge[l] coat.
7. The fixings of the fairleads, cleat[s] and block mountings should b[e] checked by gripping the fitting an[d] twisting. There should be no sideway[s] movement.

Wash the boat, its parts and fittings.

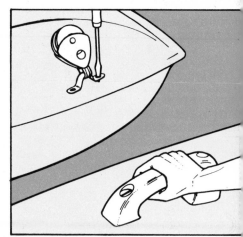
Check fittings and their fixings.

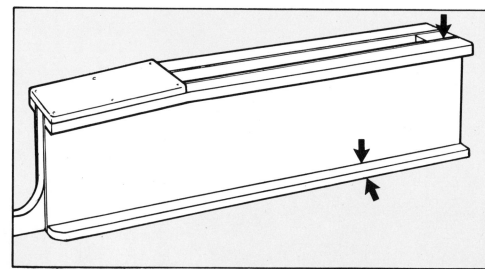
Glance at the glue join on the centrecase for signs of potential trouble.

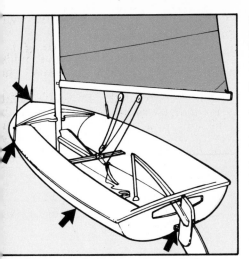

Check over the hull, also rigging links.

8. Check rigging links before and after sailing.

9. Examine the hull for scratches and flaking paint that may require touching up. Deep scores will need more than touching up.

10. Polish the gel coat on GRP boats every two months.

After every third or fourth outing turn the boat on its side to examine the bottom. Roll it over on the grass, removing any stones beforehand, and place the inverted trolley over the tip of the mast to prevent the boat from rolling back. Then make the following checks:

1. Draw out the centreboard to check for any restrictions. A pebble could wear a hole through the side of the centrecase, if not spotted.

2. Examine the centreboard closely for longitudinal splits near the bottom edge and horizontal cracks near the hull.

3. The slot closure requires replacing regularly. If torn it will allow stones to enter, the case, and cause drag.

4. Inspect the keelband and bilge rubbers if fitted. Make sure there are no jagged edges, and check for wear or cracking in the paintwork.

5. If the boat has a skeg, check for any play in it, and refix if necessary.

6. Examine the mast and rigging (*see* **Spars** and **Rigging**).

Turn the boat on its side to examine the bottom and the centreboard for problems.

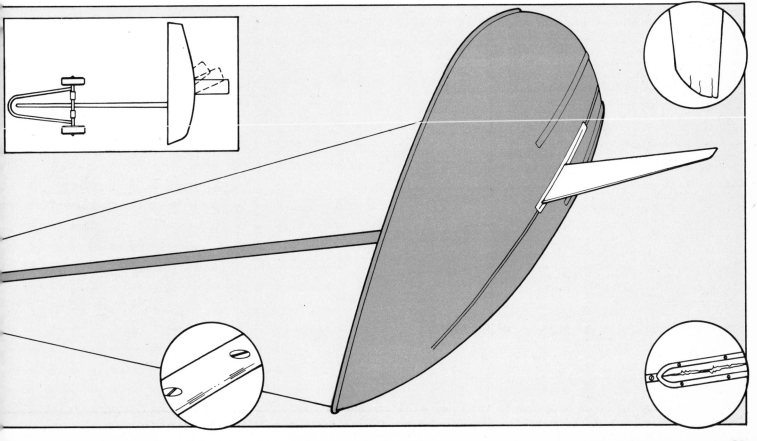

PARTS THAT GET MOST WEAR

The main stress points on a dinghy are the mast step, the transom, the side seats and thwarts. Check these regularly. Do not ignore warning signs. Problems not dealt with quickly will get worse. The centrecase, centreboard, rudder and mast also get much wear (*see* Index).

Transom The strains transmitted through the transom by the rudder are immense. Watch the screws and bolts holding the rudder fittings. If the screw holes are worn, replace the screws with larger gauge ones or preferably bolts. If the bolts enter a buoyancy tank, they must be sealed. Use a rubber 'O' ring as a second washer or set the bolts in resin or paint.

If you are going to fit an outboard motor to your boat, make sure that there are solid timber quarter knees to support the transom to the side or side tank panels. You can make these from a straight short plank of grain mahogany. Make sure that the grain runs in the right direction. A strong back should also be fitted to the inside of the transom to take the thrust of the motor. On GRP boats fit a plywood pad to the outside of the hull. Make a thin plywood pad on rubber or canvas to prevent the outboard motor clamps digging into the transom.

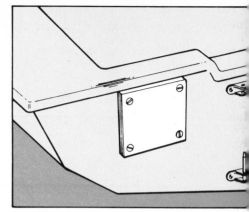

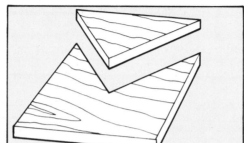

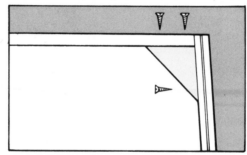
Make solid timber quarter knees.

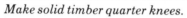
Fitting quarter knees.

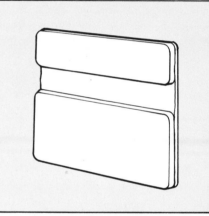
On GRP fit a plywood pad.

A thin plywood pad for outboard motor.

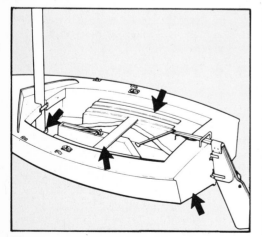
The main stress points on a dinghy.

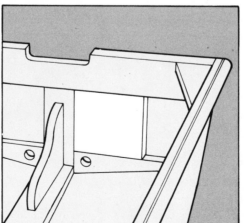
Fit a strong back inside the transom.

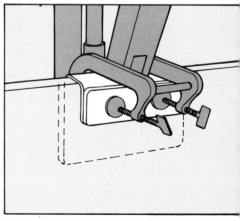
Pad protects the transom from cramps.

Check regularly for black stains or cking on the outside of the boat ere the bottom panel joins the nsom panel near the centre of the at. On wood if the varnish cracks, ape off immediately and force glue ck into the join. On GRP apply an xy fillet (see **Fastenings**), which is o good for strengthening wood. On od seal the end grain of the ply with e or epoxy.

If the buoyancy tanks extend to the ck of the boat and the fixing points of e transom are not sufficient, this ld cause leaks. If leaks are difficult cure in the conventional way (by re-ing), you should apply resin and e over the join.

On GRP look for crazing around the corners and the rudder fittings. If it urs, remove and replace the glass e around the central pillar.

eck for black stains or cracking.

Mast Step On boats with aluminium masts the heel will grind away at the wooden mast step. The hardwood plugs on the bottom of the Mirror mast will do the same. This action will chafe the varnish, strain the shroud wires, and the wood of the step will eventually be crushed.

To prevent this happening screw a stainless steel or tufnol plate on top of the step. Check first that this will not infringe the rules of your Class Association. Make sure too when you buy the plate that it will fit the heel of your particular mast. If the step is worn, skim off the top $\frac{1}{8}''$ (3 mm), seal the bare wood with varnish and fix the covering plate.

Watch also for drainage. Water will collect in the hollow of the step and eventually the wood will suffer. Apply a coat of resin to the well of the step, and if feasible drill a drainage hole through the bottom of the step and out through the side.

Side Seats and Thwarts If the seats and thwarts are used for getting in and out of the boat, the screws will work loose, water will penetrate the screw holes and the wood will become soft. On most boats seats and thwarts are not glued (to facilitate removal of the centrecase). Once the wood around screw holes is affected, larger or longer screws may hold only for a while. The best solution to the problem is to drill a pilot hole the same length as the screw. Open the hole up for two-thirds of the depth of penetration and then fill with an epoxy filler (see **Fastenings**). Fix the screw into the hole so that it stands upright until the epoxy has set. A thread will thus be formed in the epoxy so that the screw should not work loose again. Where screws have been countersunk through the seat apply varnish into the hole prior to screwing, so that water will not attack the exposed edges should the screws work loose again.

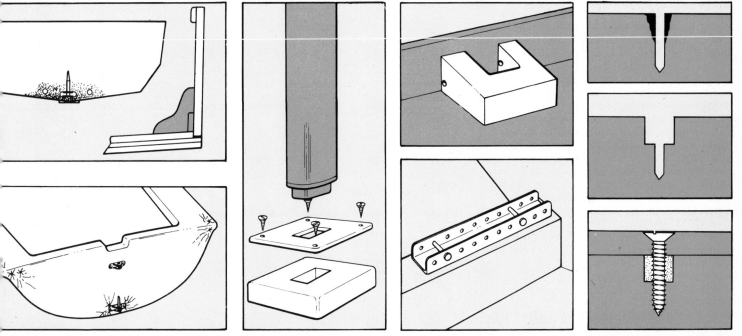

eck for crazing on GRP.　　*Fitting tufnol plate.*　　*Watch for drainage.*　　*Treating old screw holes.*

TOUCHING UP

Crazing, scores, chips or flaking paint or varnish will be spotted in your routine inspections. First clean and thoroughly dry the area, and then restore the surface.

Preparation is all important. Fresh coatings will not adhere to dirt, grease or polish. If only the top coats are affected, primers are not necessary. If damage is not due to impact or scuffing, try to discover the reason. If the surface is flaking due to suspected contamination, sand down, wipe over with a suitable solvent, and allow to dry before coating.

Wood The following directions are for the use of conventional paints using white spirit as their solvent. If you use a two part polyurethane system, apply a polyurethane primer to untreated surfaces and follow the directions for GRP below.

Clean the area, scrape off loose paint or varnish. Sand with 150 grit and taper the edges so that the fresh material will blend. If back to bare timber, the first coat of primer or varnish should be thinned with 15%-20% white spirit. The second coat should be thinned about 5%. Build up dents on painted surfaces with filler, applied after the second coat of primer. For small scratches use trowel cement. Fill deeper indentations with waterproof stopper. Slightly over-fill and sand back flush when hardened. Apply two coats of undercoat and a topcoat, sanding with 220 grit prior to each coat. Build up dents on varnish with coats of varnish until level with the surrounding area.

GRP surfaces can be touched up with paint or gel coat resin. Wash the area and clean out the groove with sandpaper. Remove loose or flaking material. Sand with 220 grit and wipe with acetone (warning: too much acetone can damage glassfibre). Shallow scores or crazing caused through impact can be filled with gel coat alone. Knife in pigmented gel coat, taking care not to trap air bubbles. On vertical surfaces stick cellophane over the gel coat to prevent slips.

If painting the surface, apply a coat of glassfibre primer directly onto the glassfibre, not to painted surfaces. Primer must be over-coated within 6-24

Check regularly for flaking paint.

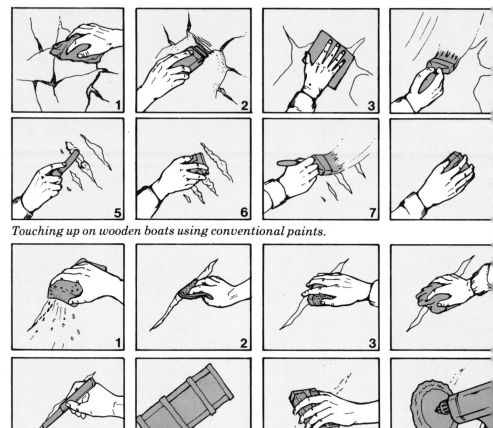

Touching up on wooden boats using conventional paints.

Touching up on GRP boats using gel coat resin.

ours with either conventional under-
oat or two part polyurethane finishes.
hen fill as necessary. Over under-
oats use trowel cement or waterproof
topping. Over polyurethane use a
olventless epoxy filler. Note that
poxy filler does not shrink as it cures,
o finish flush with the surface. Sand
ith 220 grit. Apply one more coat of
onventional undercoat and one
opcoat, or at least three more coats of
olyurethane. Sand dry with 220 grit
rior to each coat.

It is a good idea to assemble a First
Aid box for touching up and emergency
repairs:
Wooden spatulas for mixing glues etc
Brushes – 1″ (25 mm) and 2″ (50 mm)
Mixing pots
Small tin varnish, primer, paint
Small tin resin and catalyst
Self-adhesive tape – 10 yards (10 metres)
Epoxy adhesive
Waterproof glue for wood
Waterproof wood stopper/polyester
filler

Brass panel pins – ¾″ (20 mm)
Sandpaper – 60, 100, 150, 220, 400 grit
Sharp cutting knife
Plywood patches (useful also for
mixing adhesives)
Suitable solvent

*Note: resins have a shelf life of six
months. Store away from direct
sunlight and do not allow to freeze.*

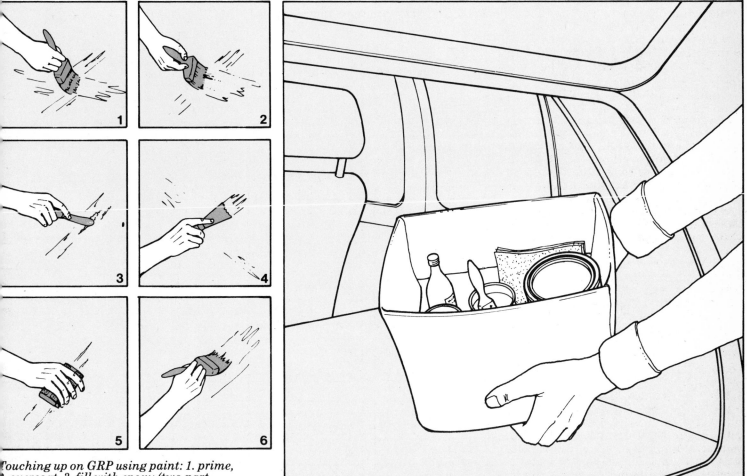

*Touching up on GRP using paint: 1. prime,
2. overcoat, 3. fill with epoxy (two-part
polyurethanes) or 4. fill with trowel cement
(conventional paints), 5. sand, 6. overcoat.*

Take a 'First Aid' box in the car boot when you go sailing.

EMERGENCY REPAIRS

The repairs described in this chapter are only temporary. They are quick and simple to do, and will enable you to sail the following or even the same day. The materials required (*see* previous page) can be carried in the car whenever you go sailing.

The first stage of any repair is to dry and clean the affected area thoroughly. A propane blow lamp can be used to dry out exposed edges on wood, but never on GRP or synthetic materials. A hair dryer is good for damp, but not wet, surfaces.

Deep Scores If the timbers on wooden boats are split, do not remove any of the damaged wood, but try to glue the pieces back into position. Cutting away the veneers will make a simple scrape into a hole. Clean the rut with 60 grit paper and remove any rough edges. Then sand with 100-150 grit and apply a coat of primer or varnish thinned with white spirit about 15%. This is to waterproof the timber. If a polyurethane system has been used on your boat, use a suitable primer thinned to the manufacturer's instructions. On a warm day you can apply a second coat within a few hours. Then fill the score. With conventional paint use a waterproof stopper and cover with undercoat. When dry sand with 220 grit all around the area and apply a topcoat. With polyurethane use a solventless epoxy filler and apply further coats of polyurethane paint.

On GRP boats sand down the score, clean with acetone and dry. Sand with 220 grit and apply a coat of resin to waterproof the glass mat. Fill with polyester body filler, finishing it flush with the surface. Sand down until smooth with 60-100 grit and then with 220. Apply a coat of resin or gel coat and touch up with paint as necessary. If the laminations are split, do not attempt to make a temporary job.

Holes and Splits can be a problem, as damage is mainly caused while sailing and the area is saturated with water. If damage is above the waterline, the boat can be used the same day by covering the area with a self-adhesive plastic tape with a good bond (Fablon). Put a patch on each side, making sure that it completely covers the affected area. Remember to remove the tape as soon as possible to allow ventilation.

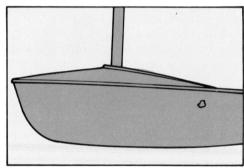
Hole above the water line.

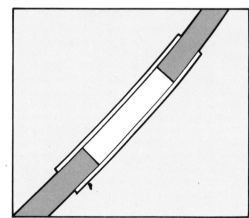
Using tape either side of the hole.

If damage is below the waterline, use a plywood patch which is ½" (12 mm) larger all round than the hole.

Lay this on the outside of the hull and mark around the patch onto the hull.

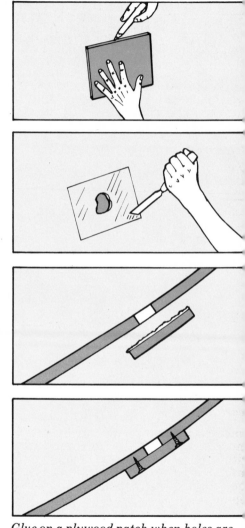
Glue on a plywood patch when holes are below the waterline.

Clean the area. On wooden boats remove the paint down to bare timber. On GRP sand the gel coat and remove all traces of polish. Glue on the patch with a quick-drying epoxy adhesive and apply pressure until the adhesive has cured. If you can reach the inside of

...he boat, seal the exposed edges and the ...nside of the pad with resin, or if the ...ole is small, with epoxy adhesive.

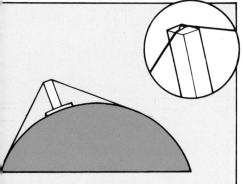

...simple way of applying pressure.

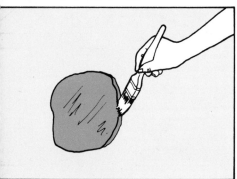

...eal edges and inside.

...ound the leading edge of the patch, ...nd taper the aft edge to reduce drag ...ith a chisel or plane. Do not make the ...atch larger than necessary, as this ...ould affect the type of permanent ...epair required.

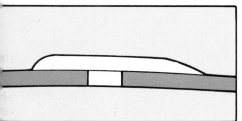

...ound off leading edge.

Cracks should not be made worse by cutting away original material. With wood push the two edges away from each other and apply glue to each edge. Press back into place. Cut a shallow 'V' along the crack on the outside of the hull and fill with adhesive. When dry, sand and seal with primer and paint.

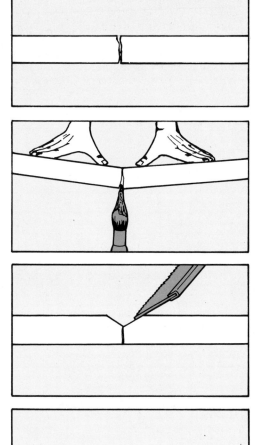

Cracks on wood.

With GRP sand and clean on the inside of the boat first. Score out a narrow 'V' on the outside skin. Apply a layer of resin and tape across the crack on the inside, and fill up with resin or gel coat on the outside. Resin and tape can also be applied to wooden boats in emergencies, provided the surface is clean and dry.

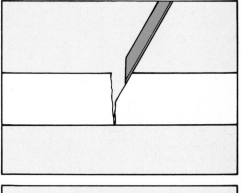

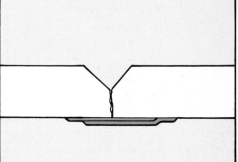

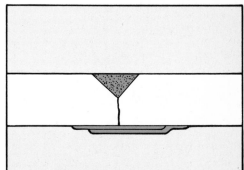

Cracks on GRP.

CARE AND CLEANING

Cloth manufacturers and sail makers have made big strides in the development of material and in sail design. Care in the handling and maintenance of sails is important in order to retain their qualities.

Sails will keep their shape providing the fibres of the cloth are not stretched and the resin finish is not damaged. Break new sails in gently, and do not use in strong winds. Do not leave sails flapping needlessly. Never pull down

Do not leave sails flapping.

sails by the leech, which is the weakest part. Overtensioning of the cunningham and clew controls can stretch the mainsail out of shape. Always hoist

Always pull down sails by the luff.

sails head to wind, otherwise you could strain the mainsail. If the sails stick as you hoist, find out the reason. If the luff is too tight in the groove, apply a candle to the bolt rope.

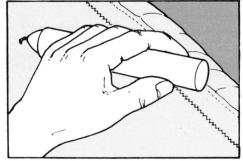

A candle will stop the luff from sticking.

Take care never to crease sails. If they do become creased, do not iron. The heat will cause the fibres to shrink. Just wash with fresh cool water and drip dry.

Fold or roll sails in the boat or on long grass. Never pull them over mud, concrete or stones. Mainsails can be folded by flaking in two or three foot (75-100 cm) widths, parallel to the foot. Try to avoid folding in the same place each time. Very stiff sails should be

loosely rolled from the head downwards. If possible roll the mainsail on the boom and then slip into the bag. Otherwise wrap the sail round a length of plastic drainpipe.

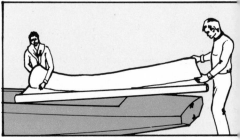

Folding the mainsail on the boom.

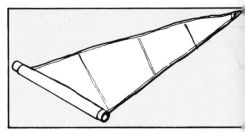

Folding the mainsail on a drainpipe.

Foresails with wire luffs should be loosely coiled along the luff, and then rolled back to the clew. Never fold the windows in sails. Spinnakers do no require special folding, but should be carefully stowed.

Do not stow sails that are still wet. Remove from the bag and leave in a dry well-ventilated place.

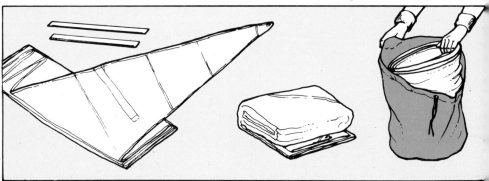

Never fold the mainsail on rough or stony ground.

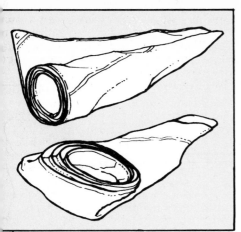

Foiling foresails.

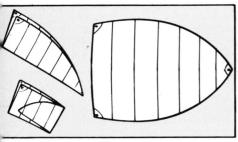

Folding the spinnaker.

If you sail on the sea, wash the sails regularly to remove the salt, paying particular attention to corners where salt gets trapped in the double layers of material. Wash the sails in a bath of

Soak stained sails in the bath.

lukewarm water with liquid detergent. Soak and then handwash. Scrub stubborn dirt with a nylon nailbrush and detergent. Rinse well and hang out to dry. Do not use tumble dryers, as the heat will damage the sails. Hang sails by the luff, tying down the clew to stop flapping. If short of space, hang from a window, tying the sail away from the wall.

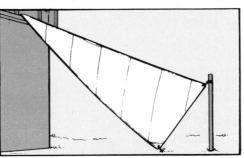

Removing tar.

Hang sail from window to dry.

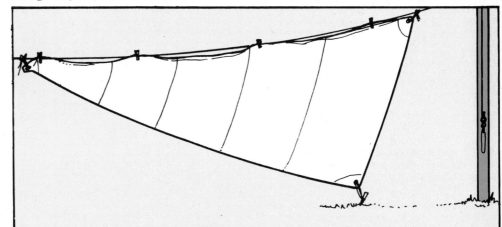

Suspend sail on washing line from the luff.

If sails become soiled or stained, wash them as soon as possible. Stains not dealt with immediately are more difficult to remove. In some cases it may be necessary to use stronger remedies. Use only milder agents on nylon and coloured sails. Wash sails after using chemicals. If in any doubt, consult the sailmaker. Here are some suggestions.

Mildew Although unsightly, this will not damage a synthetic sail, but it is a sign of poor storage. Soak the sail for two hours in a solution of ten parts water to one part household bleach. Rinse at least three times in fresh water.

Oil and Paint Attack while still fresh. Rub in a suitable gel hand cleaner (Swarfega), and leave for 10-15 minutes. Never use paint stripper. Wash out thoroughly using liquid detergent and rinse.

Blood Apply a solution of water and ammonia, using $\frac{1}{2}$ cup ammonia to 4 litres (1 gallon) of water.

Rust Brush on a solution of 25 gm (1 oz) oxalic acid dissolved in 757 ml (1 pint) hot water. Do not use on nylon. Do not allow to contact metal fittings or wires.

Tar Use white spirit, working from the outside of the stain to the middle.

REPAIRS

Many sailmakers offer a fast repair service and an end of season valet service. However, there are plenty of ongoing checks to make on sails.

As the continuous stitching on modern sails stands proud of the material, it is easily snagged or chafed. Look along the seams for broken threads when putting away the sails. Deal with these immediately or the whole seam will come unstitched. Try to find the cause of any broken threads, and if there is any chafing prevent any more occurring (*see* **Spars**).

On the mainsail check all three corners and the bolt rope at the head. Check the material below the headboard for cracks. Replace any distorted cringles. If a cringle is pulling away from the sail, reinforce it with a ½″ (12 mm) wide woven tape. Pass the tape through the cringle and sew it onto the sail lining it up with the direction of strain. Check the batten pockets along the bottom seam near the mouth of the pocket as well as the inboard end. On loose footed mainsails check the stitching in the middle of the foot where it flaps against the boom.

If the mainsail has a sleeve luff, watch for chafing at the head. Replace the webbing crown if it is worn, but a leather cap will last longer. Check the stitching down the luff seam every time the mast is threaded into the sleeve.

The main stress point on foresails is around the clew. Check the leech seam. If the edge is not sewn, look for fraying. Seal if necessary, or in bad places reinforce with a sewn patch. Check the stitching around the window.

If your sail has a wire luff, make sure that the sail is firmly fastened to it. Look for discoloration of the sail cloth, check the wire for kinks, broken strands or distorted eyelets. If you find any faults with the wire, return the sail to the makers. If your sail has hanks, check the fixings for distortion and for any faulty clips which could cut into the sail. Examine the material for signs of pulling or tearing.

The stitching on spinnakers should be checked regularly. The main stress points are the downhaul patch and the three corners.

When repairing sails you should use the same needle holes if possible. Tears and holes should then be squared out. Cut into the corners of the hole so that the edges can be turned back to form a hem. Cut out a patch, which should be the same weight of cloth as the sail, but about three times larger than the hole. Stick the patch to the sail with double sided adhesive tape. Finish by sewing around the edge of the hole and the outside edge of the patch.

When reinforcing batten pockets sew a patch onto each side of the sail but make the patches different sizes. If fitting a patch close to the luff continue the patch around the luff rope.

Sail numbers and insignia are a common cause of aggravation. When self-adhesive vinyl numbers peel off do not try to stick them back. The more expensive polyant numbers form a better bond and last longer. Do not sew numbers onto synthetic sails, as the needle holes hinder performance. Draw numbers onto spinnakers with a waterproof marker. Before sticking on new numbers clean off the glue left by the old numbers with acetone. Wash the sail as directed and ensure it is dry and free of dirt. Numbers should be fixed parallel with a seam. Allow the adhesive to cure completely by not using the sail for five or six days.

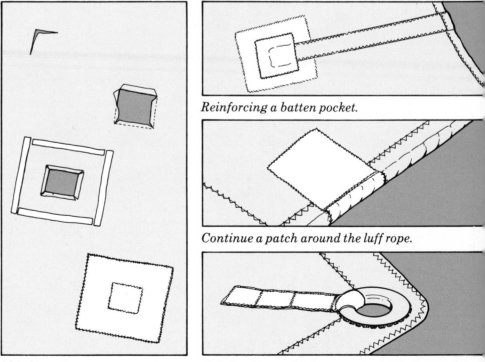

Mending a tear.

Reinforcing a batten pocket.

Continue a patch around the luff rope.

Reinforcing a cringle.

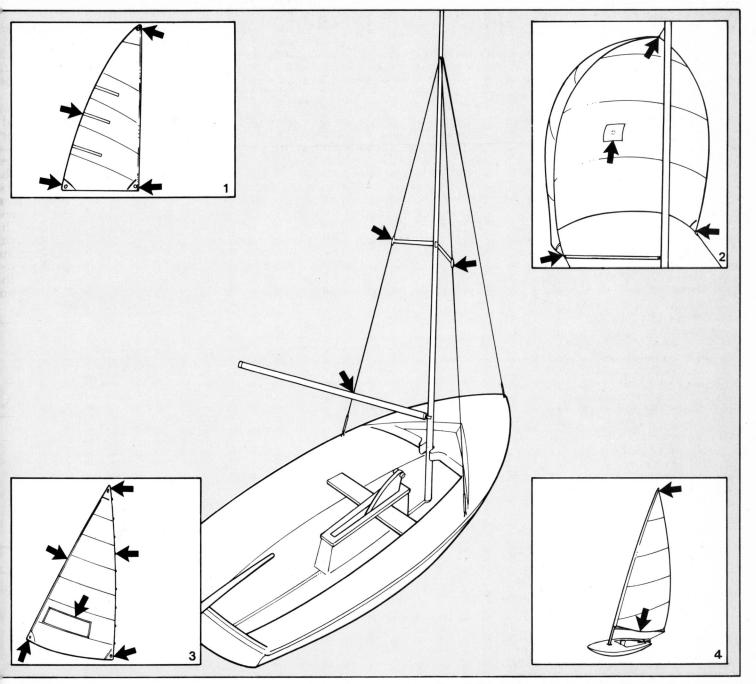

Check points: 1. mainsail, 2. spinnaker, 3. foresail, 4. loose footed sleeve luff mainsail. Remember that spars can chafe sails (centre).

CARE AND MAINTENANCE

Carry out periodic checks of the spars as well as the hull, and examine all fittings for wear. The main stress areas on the mast are the mid span between the hounds and the gooseneck. On the boom the kicking strap, tack and clew fittings should be inspected regularly.

Check for corrosion around the fixing points of the fittings. The first signs are a white powdery substance. If necessary, replace screws or rivets with a larger gauge of fixing.

Sheaves need regular attention, since they are the main cause of halliard failure. If the block wheel does not turn, remove the sheave and apply a thin oil or petroleum jelly to the axle. (This same oil is bad for synthetic ropes and sails, so use it sparingly.) Worn or sloppy sheaves should be replaced, or the halliards will jam. Use metal sheaves for wire halliards and nylon ones for rope halliards.

If you have an old wooden spar, check the centre glue join constantly, especially around the heel and gooseneck. If it breaks away, cut a 'V' into the join and fill with an epoxy adhesive. Bind with a strong polyester waxed twine if below the luff groove. If the weakness is above the start of the luff groove, through bolt.

Aluminium spars are usually supplied annodised. This finish is resistant to corrosion. In order to retain a smooth surface wash and polish with wax twice a year. Do not use abrasive cleaners.

If the spars are not annodised, frequent polishing will help to preserve them, but it is better to paint them. Degrease and remove any polish with methylated spirit and wire wool. Then apply a self-etch primer and an epoxy paint finish.

Small areas of corrosion or abrasions will not affect the strength of the spar unless they are in the high stress area. If the spar is only slightly corroded or the annodised finish has been scratched, a good coating of wax

polish will suffice. If the spar is badly corroded or the finish badly worn, gently clean the area with emery cloth and paint. If the corrosion has left holes, seek expert advice.

Minor dents in the mast at deck level indicate slack rigging. These are not serious, but it is advisable to fit doubling plates.

Bent aluminium masts can be straightened, provided there is a gentle curve and there is no crack or kink at the bend. Support the mast about 6' (2 m) each side of the bend and bounce up and down on it. Check the straightness after two bounces and remember

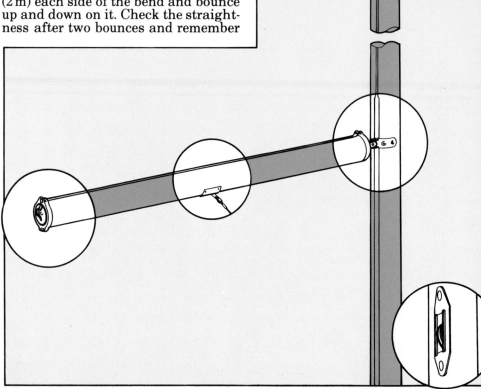

The main stress points on the mast and the boom. Check sheaves frequently.

apply sufficient pressure to bend the mast in the opposite direction so that it ill spring back. If the mast is dented r cracked at the point of bend, it is nsafe.

Luff grooves tend to open up and llow the sail to pull out, especially here the halliards run up the same ack. Close the groove by laying a iece of timber along the wall of the ack and hammering.

Wooden spars require varnishing before storing away. Never paint them. Check the screw holes first and if they have elongated, fill with an epoxy glue or a mixture of wood glue and sawdust. If possible, drill new holes in fresh timber. Where the fittings have compressed the timber, look closely for crazing of the varnish. Remove old and flaking varnish with a piece of glass, a cabinet scraper or a finely adjusted plane. Sand the luff groove and glue up any splits which could catch the sails.

If bruising has occurred, bleach the black stains out with oxalic acid (see **Have you a Problem?**). Sand timber before varnishing. Make sure the varnish does not run into the sheaves. If the heel of the mast shows signs of rot, splice to it a new piece of timber. Cut the rotten timber back to new wood. Saw diagonally for a better joint.

Check that the spinnaker boom is buoyant. If not, fill with polystyrene foam to make it float.

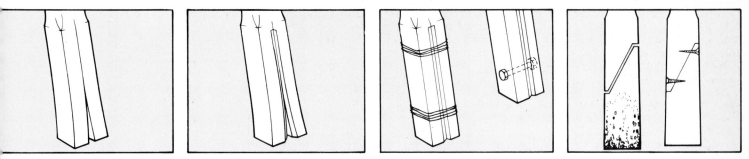

Wooden spars: If the glue join breaks, cut a V and fill with epoxy. Splicing in new timber (right).

Straightening a bent aluminium mast.

Doubling plates.

Closing the luff groove.

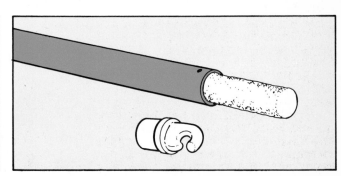

Fill a spinnaker boom which does not float with foam.

FITTINGS AND FASTENINGS

In the battle for better performance mast sections are becoming smaller. When choosing a new fitting, choose one of an appropriate size.

On aluminium spars fit only aluminium or stainless steel fittings. Fasten them on to the spar with monel pop rivets or stainless steel self-tapping screws. Ordinary aluminium pop rivets will corrode.

Avoid drilling holes in a direct horizontal line around the spar, and do not drill holes less than $\frac{3}{4}''$ (20 mm) apart in a vertical direction. For the same reason, only fit sheaves which have the fixing holes above and below the block.

If bolting a fitting in place, do not compress the wall of the mast by using mechanical advantage. Apply a coat of zinc chromate paste or a rubber based sealant to the back of a stainless steel fitting to form a barrier between the dissimilar metals. Keep self-tapping screws short to avoid fouling internal halliards.

Check the hounds fittings to make sure that the links holding the shrouds and trapeze wires are secure, and that the holes in the plates have not elongated. Check all screws. If the shrouds are hung internally, make sure the fixing tube is straight. If it is bent, replace it.

Check the spreaders and spreader brackets for stress. If they are bent or distorted, replace immediately. Make sure that the outboard ends of the spreaders are not chafing the shroud wire, and replace the binding regularly.

As spinnaker eyes and pole fixings are positioned in the high stress area, keep fixing holes to a minimum here.

Screws holding the highfield lever should be tightened occasionally, and the hinge pin checked. Check that the bearing of the gooseneck pin is not worn or distorted. If the gooseneck slips, fix a split pin through the track or

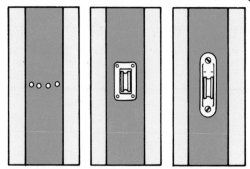

Only drill holes above and below sheaves.

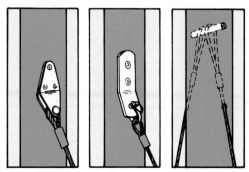

Checks on hounds fittings.

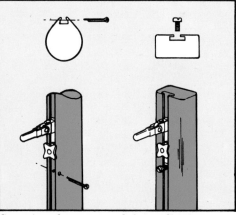

Stopping the gooseneck from slipping.

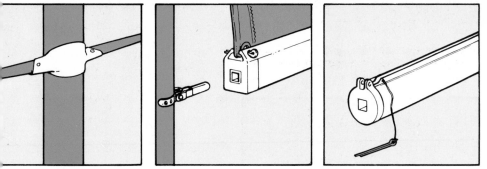

eck spreaders, gooseneck hole and tack pin.

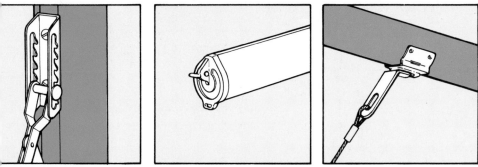

eck highfield lever screws, clew fitting and kicking strap take-off.

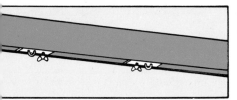

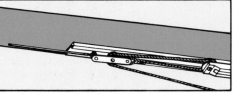

e mainsheet take-off must not foul ropes.   Check clew outhaul adjuster.

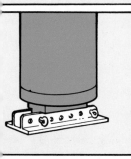

eck heel casting.

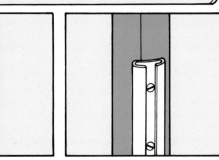

Fit new screws off centre on wooden spars.

screw a stop into the groove. The heel casting must be a tight fit. If it has become loose, drill new holes and refix.

On the boom make sure that the hole for the gooseneck is not worn. If the sail tack pin is bent, replace it. Check the lugs of the tack fitting holding the pin and the kicking strap take-off. Where the shroud wires chafe the boom in the running position, either fit pads to the boom or cover the wires with small bore polythene tube.

The sliding eyes for centre mainsheet take-offs should be at least 6″ (15 cm) apart, with their thumb screws facing each other so as not to foul the spinnaker controls. On a transom mainsheet arrangement check the end casting. If the lug holding the block has worn, hacksaw and file the lug off, and fix a sliding eye into the track on the underside of the boom. Make sure that the block for the clew outhaul revolves satisfactorily. If an internal wire is used for the outhaul, check the exit hole for chafing or corrosion. Tighten the screw clamping the wire regularly.

Too many fixing holes around the centre of the spinnaker boom will weaken it. The fittings on the end of the boom must be firmly attached. If the hook or the piston fitting is distorted, replace it.

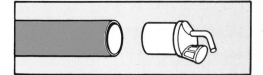

When altering wooden spars, do not position the fixing screws into the glue line of the spar, as this will weaken the join. Place the fixing off-centre. Through bolt wherever possible, and always check the fixing holes for timber rot. Never fit a tensioning lever for halliards or kicking straps to wooden spars, as the stresses are too great.

WIRES

Rigging failure is a primary cause of accidents and abandoned races. Use of the correct size and quality of wire is important. Check frequently for potential breakages. Damaged wires break very quickly.

Wires are either stainless steel or galvanized steel. Both are equally strong, but stainless steel is more resistant to corrosion. The main types of construction used for dinghies are 1 x 19, 6 x 7 and 6 x 19 with fibre core. These figures indicate the number of wires used. 1 x 19 is a single strand made up of nineteen wires. 6 x 19 is six strands made up of nineteen wires, laid round a fibre core. For standing rigging use 1 x 19 wire. It cannot be hand spliced, but its smooth exterior reduces wind resistance and is kinder to the sheets. Single strand wire has less stretch than other constructions. If hand splicing, use 6 x 7. For running rigging use 6 x 19 which is flexible and turns round small blocks without distorting. Blocks should not be less than six times the diameter of the wire. This wire can be hand spliced, either to itself or onto a rope. Trapeze wires should be 1 x 19 or 7 x 7.

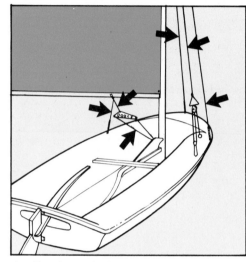

Applications of wire rigging.

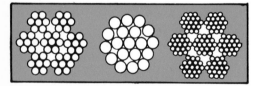

The main types of wire construction.

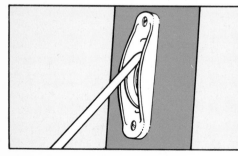

Blocks must suit the size of wire.

The normal diameter size for dinghy standing rigging is 3 mm ($\frac{3}{8}''$ c). If halliards have a rope tail, use 2 mm ($\frac{1}{4}''$ c). If they have a lever or any mechanical advantages use 3 mm. Kicking straps use 3 mm; trapeze wires 2.5 or 3 mm ($\frac{5}{16}''$ or $\frac{3}{8}''$ c). Catamarans should use 4 mm ($\frac{1}{2}''$ c) throughout.

Hand splicing wires is slow and difficult, and it is normally better to have wires mechanically spliced. One method is to bend the wire to form an eye and to swage a soft metal ferrule (copper for stainless steel and alloy for galvanized wire) around the two strands. The eye is formed around a stainless steel thimble to prevent the wire from being chafed at the bearing point. If the eye is looped over a large diameter bolt or tube, or if a rope is spliced directly onto it, a thimble is unnecessary. Another method is to fit a stainless steel terminal to the single end of the wire.

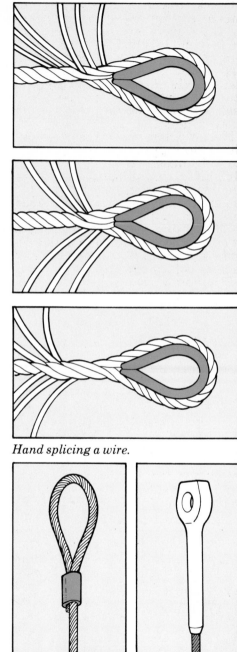

Hand splicing a wire.

Types of mechanical splice.

Check the wires frequently for broken strands or discoloration, especially where they enter a ferrule or terminal. Slide a wad of open weave cloth along the wires to detect breakages. Look for the cause of any chafing. Rust on galvanized wires is a sign of internal corrosion and eventual breakages. Stainless steel gives no such warnings.

Wash rigging with water to remove salt. If storing, rub boiled linseed oil into galvanized wires and petroleum jelly into stainless steel to preserve them. Wipe off at the beginning of the season. Always coil wires, and do not kink. When buying replacements, take the old rigging to the chandler as a pattern. Otherwise measure the length of the wire from the bearing points on the inside of the eyes.

If halliards break inside the mast,

re-threading can be a problem. Remove the sheave cages, and if the bottom sheaves are part of the mast heel remove the complete unit. Stand the mast against an upstairs window or flat-roofed building, and drop a weighted nylon fishing line down the inside of the spar. Thread the halliard tail through the top sheave and attach it to the line. Draw the halliard down the mast, hooking it out at the bottom. Thread through the lower sheave cage or mast heel. Replace the sheaves and pull halliard taut. If halliards get tangled, start again. The main halliard should always lead out of the bottom right hand sheave. Remove halliards for winter storage. Whip a thin line to the tail of the halliard and draw the halliard out from the top exit sheave. Leave the line in the mast in order to re-thread the halliard.

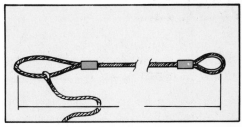

Measuring wires for replacements.

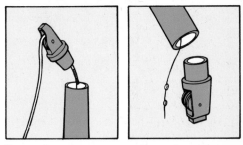

Removing sheave cages from the mast.

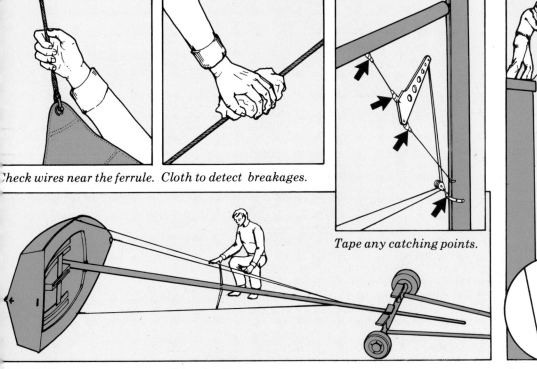

Check wires near the ferrule. Cloth to detect breakages.

Tape any catching points.

Turn the boat over to inspect all the rigging properly.

A good way to re-thread halliards.

ROPES

Choose ropes with care. They should be strong, flexible, hard wearing and easy to handle, but not too heavy or with too much stretch.

Most ropes on the market are made from synthetic fibres. Natural fibres do not have the same strength or durability as synthetics. Wash natural fibre ropes in fresh water and dry thoroughly before storing, since they are prone to rot. Wash synthetic ropes in water and liquid detergent. They will not rot, but do not store near heat. Synthetic ropes will get fluffy with wear and become easier to handle, and are recommended for sea sailing.

Ropes are constructed in a variety of ways. 3 strand ropes are made from three strands containing many filaments, twisted together to form a rope. They can be hand spliced easily. Plaited ropes are made from eight or sixteen strands woven together around a central core. If your lines are liable to twist, plaited ropes are less prone to distortion than 3 strand, but they are not as strong. Braided ropes are expensive, but most suitable for high performance dinghies. The strands of both the inner core and the outer sheath are braided. These ropes combine uniform flexibility with very high strength. Due to their low stretch they are suitable for any job and ideal for winches. They can be spliced using a fid.

Polyester is the most efficient material for dinghy ropes. It has high strength combined with low stretch. Nylon, although stronger than polyester, is not very suitable for dinghies, as it has a high stretch factor. But it is ideal for painters and lashings. Multifilament polypropylene is often used as a cheap rope for sheets. Of medium strength and with a high stretch factor, it is buoyant and good for small dinghies and painters.

For halliards on high performance boats and boats using winches use 6 mm (3/4" c) braided polyester. On most

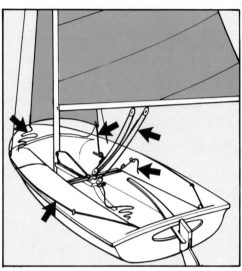

Rope rigging on a two-person dinghy.

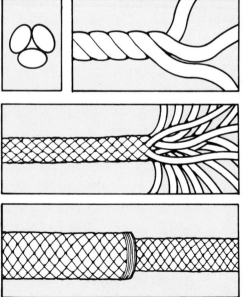

3 strand, plaited and braided ropes.

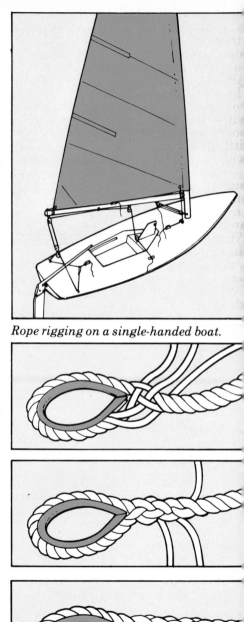

Rope rigging on a single-handed boat.

Splicing a thimble eye.

inghies all-rope halliards can be 5 mm or 6 mm ($\frac{5}{8}''$ or $\frac{3}{4}''$ c) 3 strand pre-stretched polyester, which combines high strength with low stretch. It is easy to splice an eye into this rope. Always fit a thimble to prevent the shackle chafing through the rope. If you use 3 mm ($\frac{3}{8}''$ c) wire in conjunction with a lever or hook, 4 mm ($\frac{1}{2}''$ c) polyester rope is adequate, as there is little strain on the rope. But the wire will wear through anything thinner.

For sheets use an 8 or 16 plait polyester matt finish. This finish enhances the handling qualities. On small boats use 8 mm (1″ c) diameter and on larger boats 10 mm (1$\frac{1}{4}''$ c). With control lines use 8 plait matt finish polyester for easy handling. Use mm to 8 mm ($\frac{1}{2}''$ to 1″ c) according to purpose required. Matt polyester is available in various colours for easy identification. Plastic balls knotted on

the ends of ropes give better grip.

Examine ropes carefully for wear. Check the splices or the whipping holding the eye, and apply new whipping if necessary. Check the ends of ropes for fraying. Seal the ends with a naked flame and heat shrinks, or whip with a waxed thread.

Make sure that all ropes pass freely through cleats, fairleads etc, and that they are the right size for the fitting. Examine fittings for chipped surfaces which could harm ropes. Ratchet blocks and cam cleats are particularly hard on ropes. Always allow an extra 30 cm (12″) or so on the length of ropes so that they can be moved or reversed to prevent wear.

Do not forget rope's other uses. Knots stop halliards and lines from disappearing. Use bowlines to attach sheets to spinnakers and two half hitches on blocks.

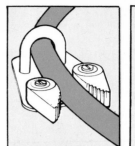

Rope too large.   *Chipped fitting.*

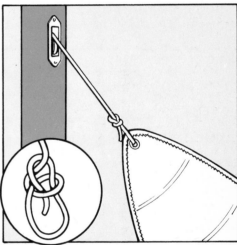

Knots: use bowlines on spinnakers.

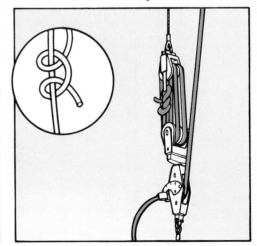

Knots: use half hitches on blocks.

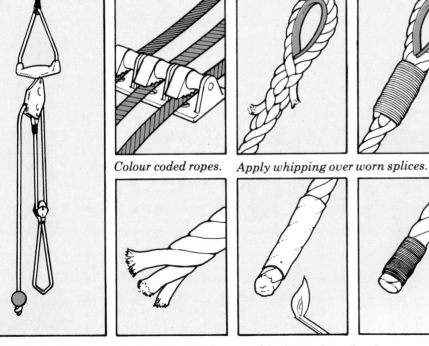

Use of plastic balls.

Colour coded ropes.   *Apply whipping over worn splices.*

Apply heat shrinks or a whipping to frayed ends.

RIGGING ADJUSTERS

There are several gadgets that enable the sails to be set to the correct tension and allow fine adjustments to be made to the rig.

Rigging screws allow extra fine adjustments. The end fittings are machined with right and left hand threads, and the barrel of the screw acts like a nut on a bolt, tensioning the shrouds as necessary. To prevent them unwinding, a locking nut is fitted above and below the barrel on some screws, or a length of stainless steel or copper wire is twisted around the screw. Check that the end of the screws are not bent or the threads damaged.

Channel type stay adjusters are lighter and more positive fixing than rigging screws. Their adjustment is not so fine, but adequate. Shroud levers give similar adjustments as stay adjusters. They are useful for slackening the tension of the standing rigging downwind. Certain Classes forbid their use. Stay adjusters and levers are available with a spinnaker fairlead and jammer incorporated.

The shrouds of some boats are shackled directly onto the chainplates. Although these are not performance boats, some kind of adjustment should be used to improve sailing and to take up any slackness that occurs in the rigging. Standing rigging can also be adjusted with lanyards spliced onto the end of wires. Use three or four turns of the rope.

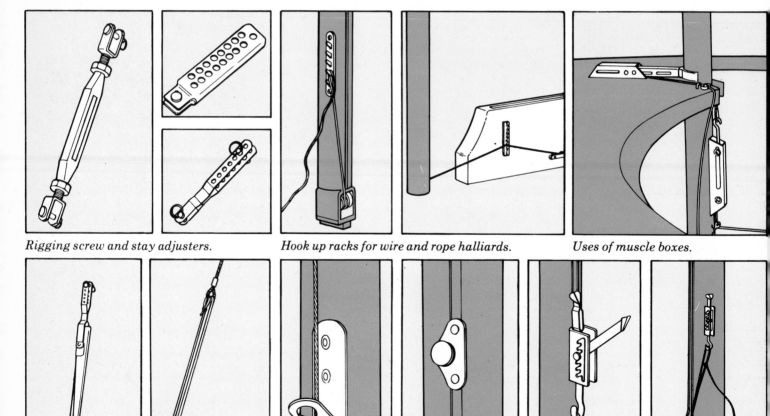

Rigging screw and stay adjusters.

Hook up racks for wire and rope halliards.

Uses of muscle boxes.

Shroud lever.

Using lanyards.

Halliard lock and button.

Highfield levers.

Hook up racks can be used on both main and jib halliards. For wire halliards screw small aluminium racks into the mast. For rope halliards fit plastic racks to the side of the centre-case. The halliard is then led aft to a cleat at the end of the case, hooking over the rack.

The eye of the main halliard can be clipped into a halliard lock fastened to the foot of the mast. When the lock begins to wear it may be difficult to disengage the halliard. An easier method of keeping the mainsail in the correct position is the hook or button fixed into the luff groove below the gooseneck. The button is fixed off centre so that the halliard does not foul other controls.

Highfield levers are for tensioning the foresail, and can only be used with wire halliards and luffs. They are normally fitted into the luff groove below the gooseneck, and can be adjusted. On deck stepped masts use the fully adjustable lever and screw permanently to the side of the mast.

Muscle boxes can be used for shroud adjustment, halliard levers and mast rams. Check that they do not allow ropes to jump off the sheaves. The pad of the mast ram should be as large as practical. Lubricate axles and slides with petroleum jelly.

Shackles etc are described elsewhere (see **Fittings**).

Emergency Repairs Always carry 2 m (6 ft) of 4 mm ($\frac{1}{2}$" c) rope in your pocket for use in emergencies. If a halliard breaks, tie the sail head to the mast. Use the line to replace lost clevis pins or shackles, to replace broken toe strap webbing or jib sheet fairleads, to tie up the centreboard or to rig up a second sheethorse.

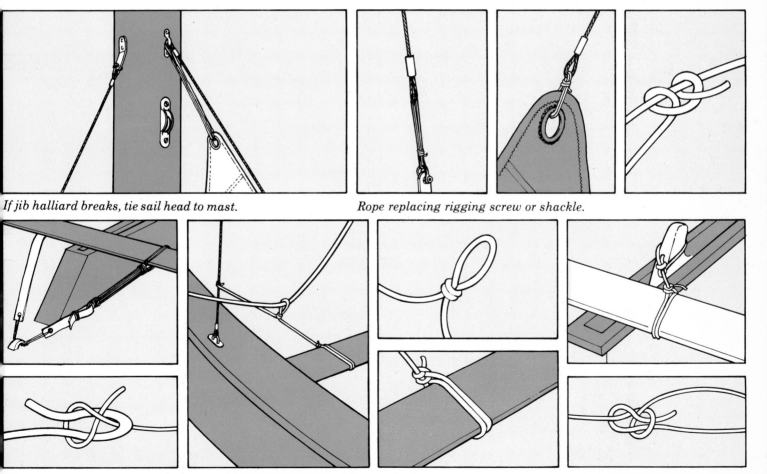

If jib halliard breaks, tie sail head to mast.

Rope replacing rigging screw or shackle.

Replacing toe strap webbing.

Rope replacing jib sheet fairlead.

Tying back the centreboard.

WHAT TO CHOOSE (1)

Fittings should be ready to hand, move freely and be readily adjustable. Fairleads, blocks and cleats should all suit their purpose, allowing sheets to work efficiently and not hindering other controls. Helmsman and crew should be able to recognize all controls at a glance.

Often screws pull out and nuts become loose because fastenings have been given insufficient support. To give the correct support, fittings must be screwed or bolted hard against the hull skin. The skin itself should have a backing pad or block fitted to give adequate fixing. These pads should be as large as possible to spread the load.

Cleats Cam cleats (1.) are available to fit most rope sizes, and are best for ropes needing continual adjustment. Nylon or plastic jaws wear quicker than metal ones, but are kinder to ropes. Metal cleats are more positive to use and last longer. Tubular jam cleats (2.) are ideal for control lines which are not heavily loaded. Serrated 'V' jamming cleats (3.) offer less windage, and do not snag ropes. Jamb cleats (4.) can be mounted separately or on the same bases as fairleads or blocks. Sometimes it may be necessary to mount cleats on angled pads.

Fairleads are mainly made of delrin and nylon. Fixed fairleads do not allow for tuning. To allow foresail adjustment choose sliding fairleads mounted on tracks. Internal tracks are made of stainless steel, and 'T' tracks of aluminium or laminated plastic. Fix with bolts and screws. Fairleads are positioned with either a plunger or thumb screws, plungers being more positive.

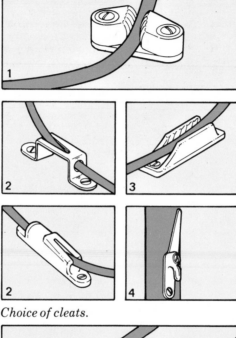

Choice of cleats.

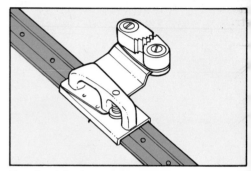

Track with plunger.

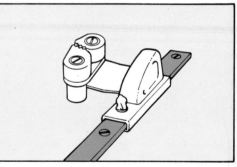

Track with thumb screw.

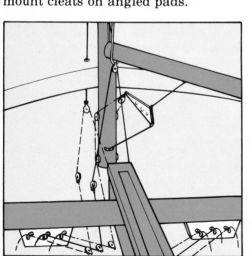

Good use of blocks and cleats for controls.

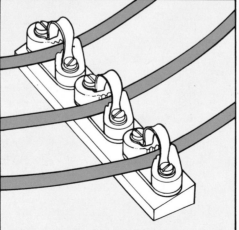

Cleats mounted on angled pads.

Internal track.

Centrecase Slot Closures Closures made from plastic film or rubber sheet require changing frequently. Fit a metal or plastic strip over them for protection. Double strength polyester sail cloth works better. Make strips longer than necessary, fasten the front end down and using holes in the aft end fasten with a line to the transom fittings. Pull taut and fix with screws using a metal or plastic strip to protect and hold flat. Curve the bands to meet at each end of the slot and cut off excess strip.

Shackles Etc Never use screw type shackles to fix the standing rigging to the mast hounds. Only use rigging links and clevis pins. The more fiddly the rings, the better. Safety pins and larger rings can be snagged.

Drop nose pins are most suitable for channel type chainplates fitted below decks. Use screw shackles where parts are removed after each sail. If used on block systems, tighten before sailing. Strip shackles have little thread, so screw extra tight. Snap shackles are useful on halliards as well as on blocks which clip onto control lines. Stainless steel hooks are handy on the end of halliards, but rather long. Safety shackles are expensive and only available in a few sizes. Swivel shackles are excellent on foresail tacks and mainsheet systems. Check the rivet for wear. Do not fit to both top and bottom mainsheet blocks. Englefield and quick release clips are ideal for the head of spinnakers. One part is fitted to the halliard and the other whipped onto the sail. Check the whipping regularly.

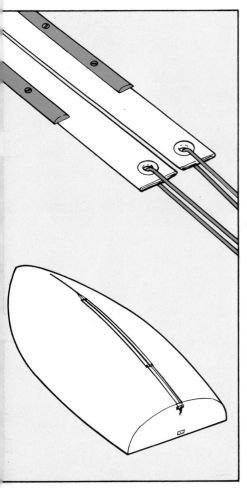

Double strength polyester for slot closures.

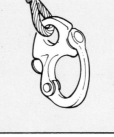

Using clevis pin at hounds.

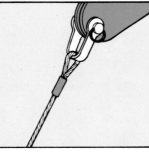

Swivel shackle.

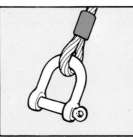

Screw shackle.

Snap shackle.

Safety shackle.

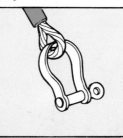

Strip shackle.

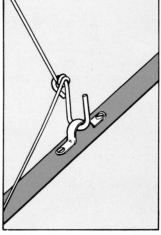

Stainless steel hook.

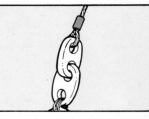

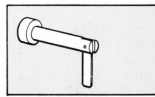

Clip, drop nose pin.

WHAT TO CHOOSE (2)

There is a very wide choice of dinghy fittings on the market. Remember that the most expensive items are not always the best for the job. Think carefully about the job you want each fitting to do and where you want to put it. Then choose the most suitable fitting, but keep it simple.

Blocks When buying blocks make sure that they suit the diameter of your rope. Standard size sheaves for mainsheet blocks are 1½″ (38 mm) diameter. Larger sheaves will reduce friction and make the sheets easier to control in heavy weather as well as easier to free in light airs. To obtain more purchase increase the number of sheaves. Small sheaves can be used on blocks mounted on a ball race, which are very sensitive even under heavy loads. Ratchet blocks will take the strain on long tacks, but they do not run very freely when spilling wind.

Do not use different size blocks or mainsheet systems. Make sure that ropes or wires leave the blocks at the correct angle and do not chafe the cheeks. In order to achieve the correct angle use the full extent of the sheet horse track and fit wire strops to the underside of the boom. Do not fit swivels to both top and bottom block or the sheets will twist.

With control lines do not allow lazy blocks to score the decks. Fit a non-tumble spring or slide a length of polythene tube over the shackle and

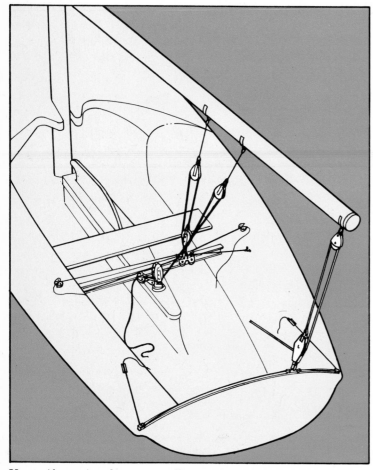

Use uniform size sheaves on all mainsheet systems.

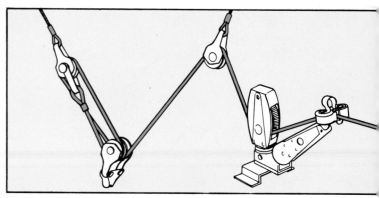

Ball bearing and ratchet blocks to increase purchase.

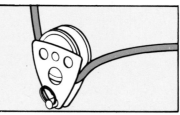

Line leaves block squarely.

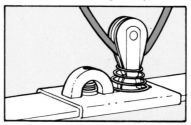

Ratchet blocks for jib.

On lazy blocks fit a non-tumble spring or use polythene tube.

ye plate. If screwing through the heeks it may be necessary to mount hem on wedge shaped pads to achieve he correct angle. Fairleads are dequate for control lines, but if ropes urn through an angle of 135° or less, se a block. When taking ropes through oles in the deck or coamings use a ylon bush.

Blocks should be used on jib sheets n large or high performance boats. Ratchet blocks are useful for trapezing rews, since they require less effort.

Spinnaker sheets are best controlled through blocks. If you use fair-leads, there is too much friction.

A block system with a cleat incorporated into the top block provides adjustment between the trapeze handle and the trapeze ring. Of the two types of handle available the triangular handle is more positive to use, while the plastic 'T' handle is smaller and lighter. If using the 'T' handle tape it to the eye in the wire to stop it revolving.

Kicking Straps Many types are available, ranging from a single purchase to levers giving a ratio of 16-1. Some Class Associations impose their own rules. If you wish to increase the power ratio on your system, check that your spars and anchor points are capable of withstanding the extra pressure. On small and medium dinghies use block systems with a purchase between 2-1 and 6-1. Fit a wire strop from the upper block to the boom, thus reducing the amount of windage. If there are proper fixings, winches are practical and uncomplicated, giving a purchase of 8-1. Levers will give up to 9-1 purchase, but this can be doubled using control lines. These can be led aft to the helmsman.

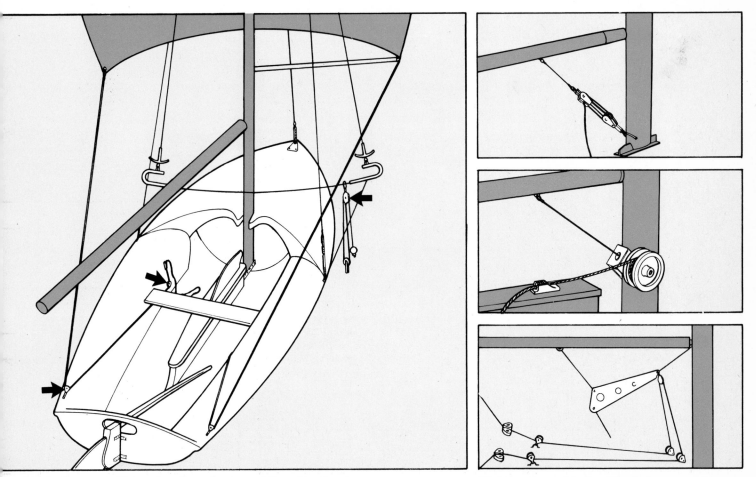

Use blocks for controlling spinnaker sheets, and for adjusting trapezes.

Kicking straps: blocks, winch, lever.

CARE AND MAINTENANCE

When checking fittings, pay attention to the fastenings. A slight gap between the fitting and the skin is a sign of fastenings coming loose. Crazing of the gel coat or paint indicates that the stresses are too much for the hull at that point. Before touching up, strengthen the hull skin.

Replace worn or distorted fittings. Relocate them if possible, filling the original screw holes. Otherwise use larger diameter screws, through bolt or drill out the screw holes and glue in wooden plugs or epoxy filler. Check all fittings regularly including shackles and rigging links. Swill out blocks and if possible apply petroleum jelly to the axles. The following fittings get most wear:

Chainplates Check for crazing on the surrounding hull skin. Check fastenings, clevis pins and holes to which shrouds are attached for distortion. Check plates for cracking and twisting. Check rigging adjusters. If there is an accident resulting in broken shrouds, replace chainplates even if they appear undamaged.

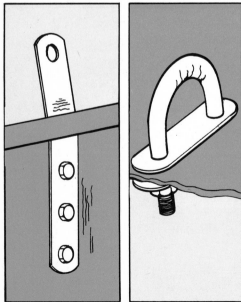

Checks on chainplates.

Rudder Fittings Always bolt if possible. Pintles and gudgeons will twist if fastenings work loose. Look for cracks and loose pintle pins in cast aluminium fittings. With strip stainless steel fittings check the welding, look for distortion, and cracks across the screw holes. If the pivot bolt for the blade shears or the nut becomes loose, the cheeks of the stock will splay. Keep the nut tight, and burr the thread with a nail punch.

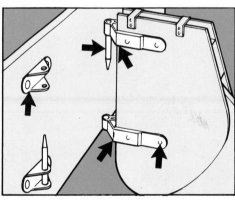

Checks on stainless steel rudder fittings.

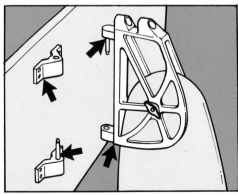

Checks on aluminium rudder fittings.

Tiller Wear of the ball joint or pin of the universal joint on the extension will cause slackness and affect the response of the tiller. Replace the rubber joint at the first signs of splitting. Renew cotter pins frequently

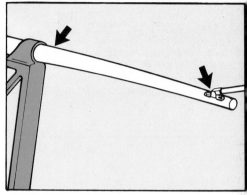

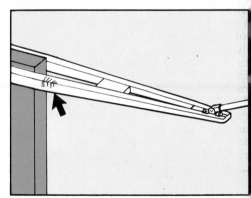

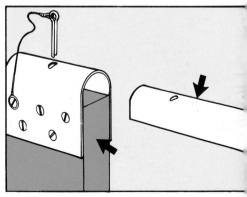

Checks on tiller stress points.

Stemhead Watch principally the horizontal fastenings. Check pins and attachment points for wear.

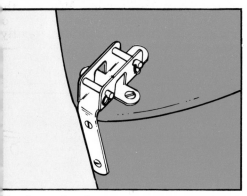

Check stemhead screws.

Tracks Fasten foresail tracks alternately with bolts and screws. Do not allow deposits to collect in the grooves. Wash and lubricate with aerosol polish. If the fairlead slide uses the plunger type of lock, clean out holes of the track. If a thumb screw is used, tighten before each sail and check track for wear. On internal tracks check for damage or opening of the track and wear on the slides. On centre mainsheets using 'X' track or stainless steel tubes replace worn rollers on the traveller and check take-off points.

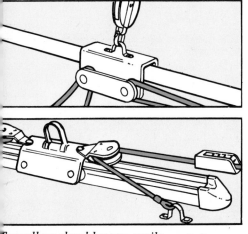

Travellers should move easily.

Cleats Wash to stop deposits building up. If cam cleats can be dismantled, fit replacements. 'V' jamming cleats require little maintenance. Check plastic tubular jam cleats for splitting. Check screws or rivets and feel for play on the fastenings of conventional cleats.

Keel Bands and Bilge Rubbers Check metal strips for cracking and bending, especially across screw holes. Plastic strip is normally glued or pinned to the hull. Cut if damaged and fix a screw or pin $1/4''$ (6 mm) in from where you cut, and replace short lengths.

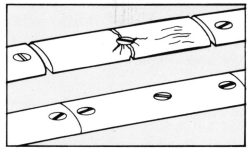

Replacing section of keel band.

Spinnaker Chute Check for rough edges. If grooves are caused by the halliard, reinforce with glass tape. Fill dents or cracking in the gel coat. Renew the mastic sealing the chute every two or three seasons. Polish regularly to reduce friction.

Toe Straps Check webbing for chafing, loose stitching or fraying at the anchor points.

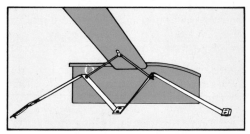

Checking toe strap webbing.

Rowlocks Look for crazing about 6″ (15 cm) below the gunwale. Fit collars to oars to prevent shafts wearing. If oars split, bind with strong tape or cap with glass tape and resin.

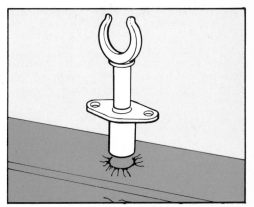

Look for crazing around rowlocks.

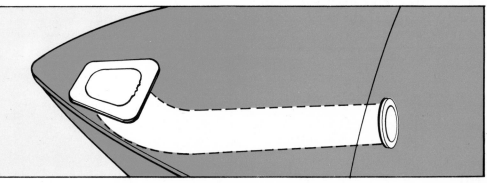

Look for splits on spinnaker chutes.

BAILERS, TRANSOM FLAPS

If you go sea sailing or racing it is worthwhile having a means of drainage. Self-bailers clear all of the water from a boat, and can be fitted in all boats, except those with a double floor. Transom flaps remove a large quantity of water rapidly, but not down to the last drop.

Self-Bailers The most popular self-bailers are the Elvström wedge-shaped chute and the Seasure 'Supersuck' which works on the venturi principle. The Supersuck requires less boat speed to remove water, but is prone to being fouled by weeds.

The bailer should be fitted to the lowest part of the boat. Avoid causing obstruction to the crew. If possible, fit it so that the thwart covers half the bailer (fore to aft) if it is positioned in front of the thwart, or with the thwart covering three-quarters of it if it is positioned behind. On V-shaped hulls fit the bailer as close to the centre line as practical without breaking into any joins. On flat-bottomed boats fit it near to the first chine, as the efficiency of the

bailer is affected by the turbulence caused by the centreboard. If the dinghy has a centre spine which restricts the waterflow, fit one bailer on either side of the centrecase.

Bailers are supplied with a pattern of the hole to be cut into the hull. Mark around this template in the desired position. The centre line of the bailer must be parallel to the centre line of the boat. If the base plate is fitted to the exterior of the hull, take care in cutting the hole on the inside of the boat and vice versa. Use a trimmer knife to cut cleanly through the outer skins. Drill a $\frac{1}{16}''$ (2 mm) hole in each corner, $\frac{1}{8}''$ (3 mm) in from the template lines. Open up the holes with a $\frac{1}{4}''$ (6 mm) bit. Using a pad saw or junior hacksaw

blade, saw along the lines marked by the template, joining the holes. Smooth off the sawn edge with a file. Lay the bailer in the hole and drill the bolt holes. If the bailer base plate is fitted to the exterior, pare off the first veneer with a sharp chisel so that the bailer is flush with the bottom of the hull. If the hull skin is less than $\frac{1}{4}''$ (6 mm) thick as on GRP, avoid doing this.

Seal the exposed edges around the aperture with two coats of varnish or resin. Apply sealing compound or rubber gasket if supplied and bolt the bailer down. Clip or saw off the end of the bolts close to the nuts, and scrape off excess sealing compound. Tighten the nuts after one week. After two or three seasons check whether the bailer is leaking. If so, renew bedding compound or rubber gasket. Make sure beforehand that you have spare bolts in case they need replacing.

Check regularly for grit which could stop the bailer from closing properly. Hose with water and clean with an old toothbrush. Do not use grease or oil, as

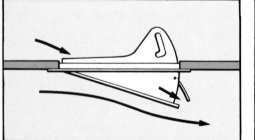
How the chute bailer works.

Possible position.

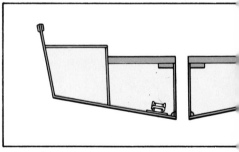
Bailer on V-shaped boat.

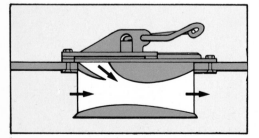
How the supersuck bailer works.

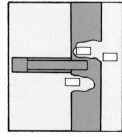
Possible position.

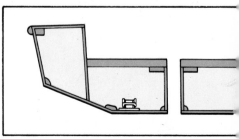
Bailer on flat-bottomed boat.

and and grit stick to the gel. During a
capsize, shut the bailer quickly to stop
the water pouring in once the boat is
righted. An open bailer is also
dangerous. If leaks are caused by
impact damage, remove the working
part of the bailer and force it back into
shape.

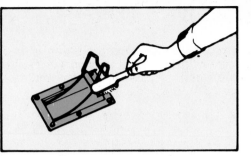

Clean bailers regularly.

Transom Flaps Transom flaps will
bail out the boat once it has reached a
reasonable speed, provided weight is
kept in the stern. Before fitting flaps,
check your Class Association rules.
The two apertures are cut into the
transom each side of the centre pillar.

Use the drill and hacksaw method
described above. Smooth the inside
edge and seal with three coats of
varnish or resin. The doors covering
the apertures are made from $\frac{1}{4}''$ (6 mm)
perspex. Anything thinner distorts
and does not create an effective seal.
Buy strong hinges, if possible cranked
stainless steel cabinet ones. Screw the
hinges to the centre pillar. If the
transom is joined with glass tape,
make the holes high enough so that the
flaps do not sit on the tape and prevent
an effective seal. The doors are held in
place with shock cord tensioned onto a
hook within easy reach of the helm.
The hook should not get in your way
when tacking. Replace shock cord
regularly as it stretches, since flaps are
never completely watertight.

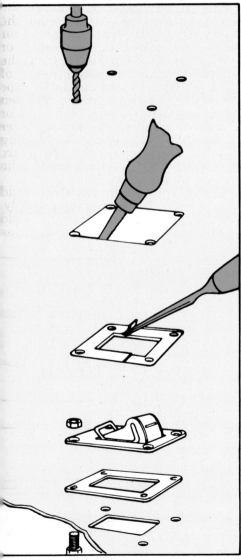

Fitting a self-bailer.

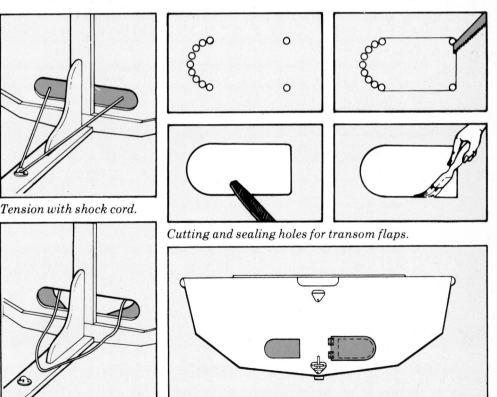

Tension with shock cord.

Hook close at hand.

Cutting and sealing holes for transom flaps.

Cut holes for transom flaps either side of the centre pillar.

FOILS

The centreboard and rudder account for a high proportion of the underwater surface area. It is therefore important to maintain the finish and to deal with knocks immediately. Any scores on wooden boards will soak up water very quickly.

Centreboards Carry out routine checks (see **Hull Care and Maintenance**). Check also the stirrup fitting fastenings. If the pivot hole is worn, renew the bush. Adjust the friction device if necessary and check its hoses or pads for wear.

When choosing a new centreboard consider the following points.

The board should be the maximum thickness allowed by your Class rules. Remember to measure the width of the slot in your boat first and deduct $\frac{1}{8}'$ (3 mm) as even slight warping can jam the board. Bush the pivot hole to reduce wear. Plywood does not warp as readily as solid or laminated timber, but is less strong and more flexible. Do not select a solid timber board less than $\frac{3}{4}'$ (20 mm) thick. While working on the board store it flat and covered. Varnish or prime as soon as possible to prevent the wood warping.

Work the board to as near an aerofoil section as possible. Taper the leading edge in slightly to a blunt bull nose and taper the aft and bottom edges to a fine (1 mm) point. Note that some Class Associations rule that boards should be flat across their section, with a taper or fairing around the edge 2-3″ (50-75 mm) wide. Certain high performance dinghies allow a full aerofoil section board. Here the thickest part should be about a third of the width in from the leading edge.

For best results stiffen the board with three coats of epoxy resin. Alternatively paint or varnish in the usual way (see **Coatings and Finishes**). A good painted surface is recommended, as it allows for filling up imperfections. Burnish the final coats to a super smooth finish.

When fitting the board into the case check that it does not stick anywhere. Extend the board fully at 90° to the boat and mark the top, three-quarter half and quarter positions in different colours or thicknesses to help you while sailing. If the board vibrates while sailing, the aft edge requires a finer taper, or the board may be too loose in the slot. If the edges get damaged splice in a new piece of timber as for rubbing beads, and mould to shape.

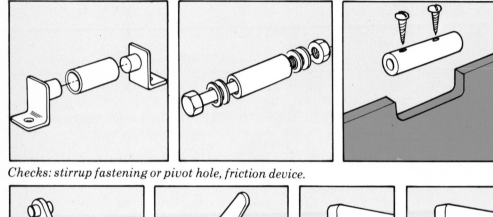

Checks: stirrup fastening or pivot hole, friction device.

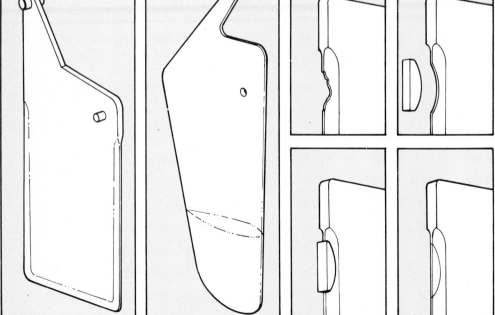

Flat and aerofoil shaped centreboards.   *How to repair a damaged edge.*

Rudders The above guidelines apply to rudder blades. However the leading edge should be slightly thicker in relation to the thickness of the material than on centreboards. Taper this edge 1″ (25 mm) above and below the line of the bottom of the transom for better water entry.

Rudder stocks should be as light as possible, but strong enough for the job. The blade should pivot easily without being loose. The tiller should have a positive fixing onto the stock, with no projections around the head for ropes to foul. The stock should fit above the water line, with the aft edge shaped to clear the water. Control lines should be positive to handle. Use separate lines for uphaul and downhaul. Use small fairleads to route them to the tiller. Replace shock cord regularly.

To fit control lines drill a $\frac{3}{8}$″ (9 mm) hole, $\frac{1}{2}$″ (12 mm) in from the edge. With a $\frac{3}{16}$″ (5 mm) bit drill into the edge of the blade down to the first hole. Thread cord into the $\frac{3}{16}$″ (5 mm) hole and out through the larger one. Knot the cord and pull back into the rudder.

Check the tiller regularly for stressing near to the join of the stock. Check the cheeks of the stock for crazing. On wooden stocks check the glue joint. On aluminium stocks check the welded joints and make sure that the wing nuts of the pivot bolt are tight but not squeezing the cheeks.

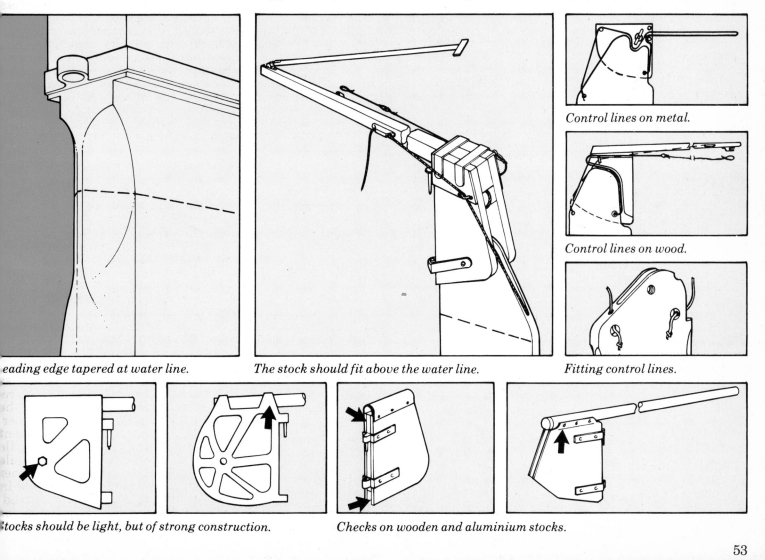

Leading edge tapered at water line.

The stock should fit above the water line.

Control lines on metal.

Control lines on wood.

Fitting control lines.

Stocks should be light, but of strong construction.

Checks on wooden and aluminium stocks.

BUOYANCY

Boat buoyancy ensures that after a capsize a dinghy with full crew aboard will be sailable. Regular checks will guarantee safety.

Buoyancy Tanks All tanks must have adequate drainage and ventilation. Provided they are dry the tanks can be used for storing spares, but remember that this will reduce the amount of buoyancy. The inside of tanks in wood or composite boats must be treated against water with epoxy or conventional primers and paint. Repair any punctured tanks straight away.

After sailing remove drainage bungs and hatch covers. Check that the tanks are dry and that the drain sockets are not blocked. On wood or glassfibre hatches check that the rubber seal is not split or perished. Renew if necessary and fix a sponge strip with a skin on both sides with a contact adhesive. Check that wood or metal turnbuttons are tight, and make a stainless steel or plastic plate to prevent the turnbuttons from wearing a groove in the hatch lid. On plastic screw types of inspection cover check the tightness of the screws regularly. Replace the rubber 'O' ring seal or mastic used for bedding in the collar when they crack or harden. Apply a thin film of petroleum jelly to the threads of the cover.

Tanks should be checked periodically for leaks. All leaks should be stopped as soon as possible. Here is a useful way of doing such a check. Make up a simple inflation tube from a length of $\frac{1}{4}''$ (6 mm) I.D. polythene tubing. Find a cork to fit the drain socket of the tanks, and drill a hole through it just large enough to take the tubing. Fit the cork into the drain socket and blow into it three or four times. As pressure builds up, resistance will be felt. Stop up the end of the tube with your thumb and release the jet of air onto your face. If there is no build up of pressure, find out where the air is escaping. Check all seams. Leaks can be heard or detected using soapy water. The best way to seal a leak is to apply resin and tape, either locally or to the whole seam (see

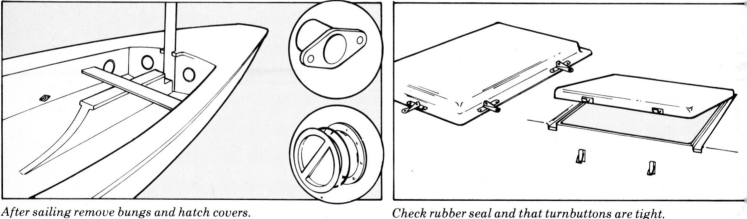

After sailing remove bungs and hatch covers. *Check rubber seal and that turnbuttons are tight.*

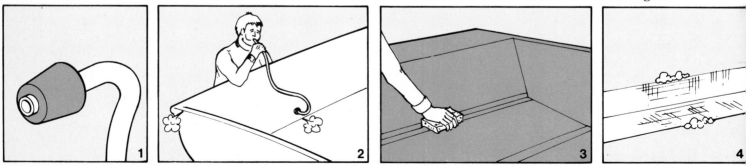

Checks for tank leaks. Place cork in tank and blow (1. & 2.). If no pressure builds up, smear soapy water over the seam (3. & 4.).

Repairs). If the leak is inaccessible, cut a hole for an inspection hatch as for transom flaps and attack the leak from the inside (one hatch per tank).

If the leaks in GRP tanks are impractical to repair (e.g. a broken deck join), fill the tank with polyurethane foam or polystyrene blocks. Do not use these materials with wood or composite boats, as they trap water.

Buoyancy Bags Each time you wash the boat swill all around the bags and under the webbing. At the end of the season wash bags and straps in warm soapy water. Roll them up and do not crease. Oil and grease will damage the materials. If you repair the hull, make sure that nothing sharp presses into the bags. Do not stretch the fabric by poking paddles and poles under the straps. If a bag has a leak, do not attempt a repair, but return it to the manufacturer.

When replacing the fixing straps inflate the bags and check that the straps are tight but not distorting the bags. Check that the screws are driven home and any burrs filed off. Use 1¼-2″ (30-50 mm) wide nylon webbing. Pillow bags less than 20″ (50 cm) require two straps and longer bags three. Stern or bow bags need one strap to hold them sideways and one lengthways. Handle carefully in cold weather as the material becomes brittle. Do not over-inflate in warm weather.

Check regularly for cracking of the material, especially around the inflation tube. Check the cap of the tube. If it has a screw thread, wash out any dirt and make sure that the rubber seal in the cap is serviceable. If a push-in bung is used, look for splits around the mouth of the tube. Do not allow dust to enter the tube. When unscrewing the cap grip the inflation tube tightly to avoid straining the bag. Check that the lugs or straps have not broken away from the bag or split. Check the straps and their fixings, and replace any frayed straps.

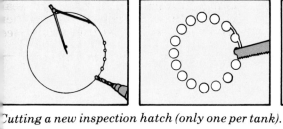

Cutting a new inspection hatch (only one per tank).

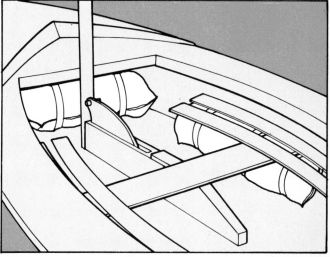

  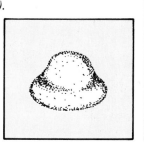

Use foam on GRP boats only.

Secure bags with sufficient webbing straps.

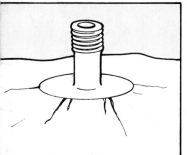 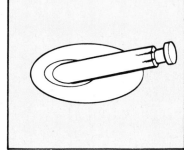 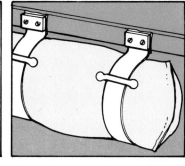 

Carry out checks on all parts of the bags.

Grip tube when unscrewing cap.

TROLLEYS

A good launching trolley will enable you to launch your boat almost anywhere. Avoid causing damage to the hull by loading the boat carefully onto the trolley and by having well designed chocks.

When loading the boat on to the trolley always tie the bows to the handle. Position the boat so that it is well balanced fore and aft with a slight bias at the front. If the boat is stern heavy, the transom will drag on the ground. If the bows are too heavy, it will be difficult to handle. Drain water from the boat before dragging it up the beach or slipway. The extra weight of water will strain both boat and crew.

The main weight of the boat must be taken by chocks or rollers under the keel. Side chocks should support the boat on the chines and bilge keels. Side chocks are also necessary to keep the boat level. Chocks should be positioned so that it does not matter if the tired crews load the boat incorrectly. They must be large enough and strong enough for your boat. If they are too small they will concentrate too much pressure in one place. If your boat does not have chines or bilge keels, chocks should be fitted or moulded to the shape of the boat to give support.

Make sure that there are no sharp edges on the chocks which could damage the boat. Canvas covered sponge pads or soft plastic tubing are ideal covering materials. Do not use old tyres, as the tread harbours stones and grit. Rollers are recommended for keel protection, but their small area makes them unsuitable for side supports. The

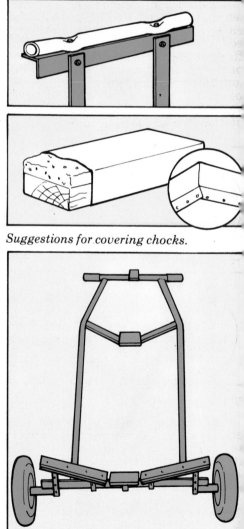

Suggestions for covering chocks.

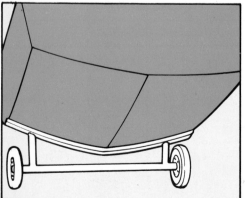

Centre the boat onto the trolley.

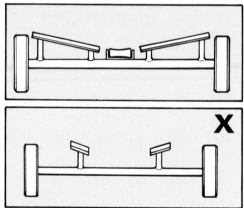

Right and wrong trolley supports.

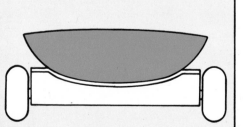

Typical moulded support.

A well designed trolley.

xle to which the chocks are fitted must e strong enough to support the boat, lus a good allowance for the weight of ater inside it. The forward support on he trolley is a cross piece attached to he handle or the handle itself. Pad hichever part comes into contact ith the boat. The 'U' shaped handle is tronger than the 'T' type and easier for entering the boat on the trolley.

Wheels are available with plastic or etal centres, and both use a plain earing. Roller bearings are un-ecessary for trolleys and are easily ffected by continual immersion. Do ot use narrow wheels. Solid tyres are ore usual than pneumatic tyres. pecial ball or cone shaped wheels are vailable for use on soft sand and mud, ut can also be used on hard surfaces.

ypes of trolley wheel.

Renew the padding on the chocks as ecessary, but also check the screws of he keel band in case they are cutting nto the material. If rubber rollers ear, their metal bracket will cut into he hull. Check the centre of the axle for istortion or corrosion. Check that the heels turn freely and grease the axles. heck that the fastenings are tight. ouch up the paint or galvanizing if ecessary. At the end of the season

strip down the trolley, emery the axles and replace split pins and washers. Grease all the nuts and threads of the bolts.

Take extra care if using the trolley with a combination trailer. Check the rubber rollers fitted to the rear of the trailer axle, and check the metal hooks on the trolley axles for distortion. Use

padding between trailer and trolley to prevent scraping.

Rollers made of rubberized canvas are useful for sandy beaches and practical to stow, but easily damaged by sharp objects. Wheels can be clipped to the transom or skeg of small light-weight dinghies and taken aboard after launching.

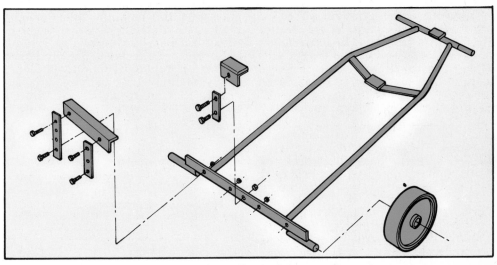

At the end of the season strip down the trolley and then store.

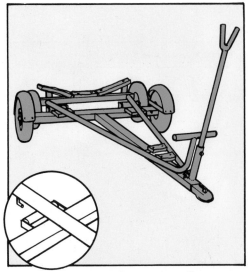

Use padding on combination trailers.

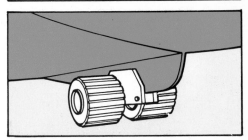

Alternatives to the trolley.

TRAILERS

Choose a trailer to suit the weight and length of your boat and allow for the weight of extra gear carried in the boat. Trailers must give better support to the boat than trolleys. Driving speeds and uneven surfaces impose considerable strain on the hull, so do not buy an inferior trailer.

On most trailers the axle can be adjusted to suit boat length. Incorrect positioning of the axle will affect the towing characteristics of the trailer and towing vehicle. The suspension must suit boat weight and length. If it is too hard, it will cause severe vibration to boat and trailer. If it is too soft, the boat could be damaged travelling over rough surfaces. The usual wheel size is 16″ (40 cm) diameter. If you make frequent long journeys with a large boat, it is better to use 20″ (50 cm) wheels, but check the legal requirements regarding brakes. A trailer should have a good bow snubber to prevent the boat sliding forward when braking. Remember that exceeding the speed limit means extra wear on bearings and tyres. Always carry a spare wheel and bearing pack, plus the correct size spanner for the wheel nuts. If you travel with an empty trailer, remove the mast carrier. Avoid immersing the trailer, but if you do, pump grease into the bearings straight away to dispel water.

Before starting a journey grease wheel bearings, check tyre treads and pressures, the locking device on the hitch, bolts on the towing bracket, wheel nuts and security pins. Tie up loose gear in the boat, distribute the weight evenly and do not overload. Carry heavy objects such as outboard motors and spare wheels in the car boot.

Secure the boat to the trailer using two straps made from 2″ (50 mm) wide webbing with a buckle or rope tails to obtain a purchase. Attach the aft strap to the take off points on the trailer axle. Take the forward strap across the foredeck, and take a line from the middle of this strap back to the thwart or aft strap to act as tensioner. If you use a travelling cover, fasten the strap over it and make taut against the wind. Pull the bows up to the snubber and tie, padding the deck to prevent chafing. Make sure that the mast carrier is secured to the trailer. Tie the mast securely at the mast carrier and at the stern, padding well. Place the ends of the rigging in a bag. The trolley can be rested upside down on the boat with the axle over the dinghy frame. Pad well. It is better to carry it on the car roof. The lightboard must conform to legal requirements. Fasten to the transom not to the back of the trailer. If necessary screw on fittings to match the transom fittings. Pad well. Never immerse the board. Carry spare bulbs. Check the cable and plug and clean regularly.

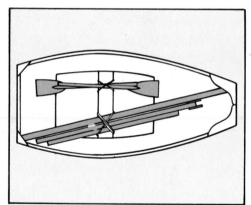
Secure spars in boat when possible.

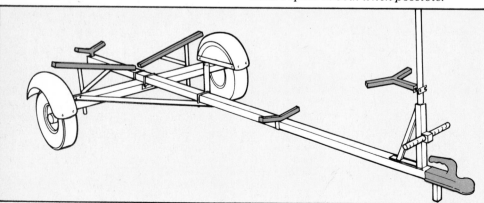
A well designed trailer.

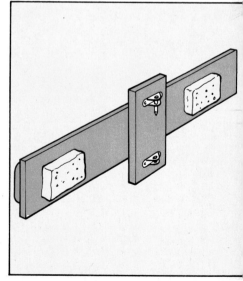
Transom fitting on the lightboard.

58

Check and grease nuts and bolts and replace if corroded. Check pads or rollers for wear as well as keel band screws on the hull. Check the stays holding the mudguard brackets for fatigue. Cover the ball bracket and grease the hitch and car bracket. Rubber suspension units are almost maintenance free, but check the nylon end caps. Grease the leaf springs and check fixing bolts. If brakes are fitted, keep correct cable tension and look for broken strands and loose terminals. Grease the blocks and lever. Check the axle for stress cracks or flexing. If storing the boat on the trailer for the winter, jack it up and rest the chassis on bricks. Remove wheels and hubs. Wash bearings and re-grease. Check paintwork and welded joints.

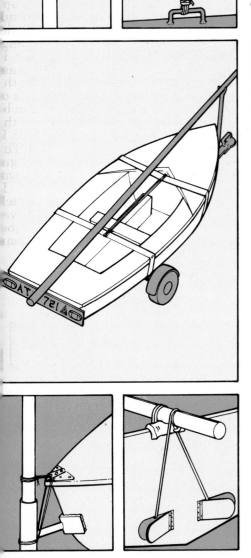

Secure the boat firmly to the trailer.

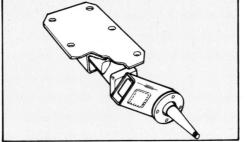

Suspension unit.

Grease the hatch and car bracket.

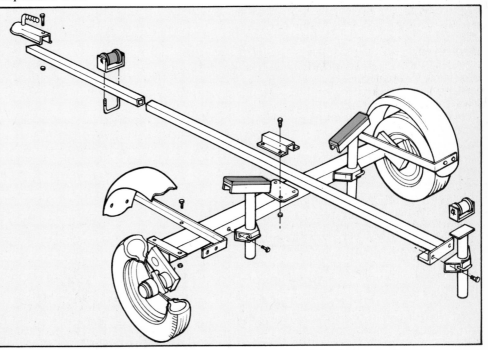

At the end of the season strip down the trailer and check all parts.

SCREWS AND NAILS

Metal fastenings are a vital part of the hull and spars. When choosing fastenings, always consider where they will be used and the likely strains. Insufficient fixings will cause stress and breakages, and bad anchorage points will prevent fastenings from gripping.

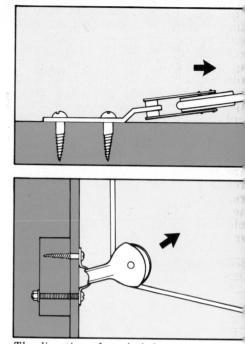

The direction of strain is important.

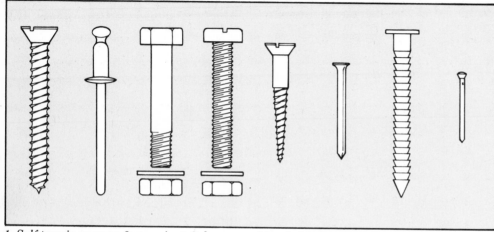

1. Self tapping screw, 2. pop rivet, 3. hexagonal headed bolt, 4. machine screw, 5. wood screw, 6. copper boat nail, 7. barbed ring nail, 8. panel pin. Numbers 1. 4. & 5. are available in countersunk, raised and pan heads.

Use only self tapping screws, rivets or bolts on GRP hulls and metal masts. Bolt rudder fittings and chainplates. Never use steel or plated steel on hulls. Use brass wood screws for panels on the bottom of wooden hulls, planking, panels which have been stressed into position and on brass fittings. Use copper boat nails or barbed ring nails on low stressed areas and varnished hulls. Use pins on deck panels which are not highly stressed.

Do not rely on a single thickness of plywood or GRP as a suitable fixing point for fittings. Build up GRP with thicker laminations (see **Repairs**) or, as on wooden boats, fit pads to spread the stresses. Choose the correct size screw or bolt to prevent movement of the fitting. On stainless steel or aluminium fittings use stainless steel fasteners, and on nylon fittings use stainless steel or brass, except for

metal spars when stainless steel must be used. Most stainless steel fittings require pan or round head screws. Fix screws at right angles to the direction of the strain imposed. If screws have to be fitted in the same direction as the strain, use the longest screws possible, or bolt. Apply varnish or resin to screw holes to waterproof the fixing point. Keep screwdrivers clean and square in the slot. Ratchet screwdrivers give screws more torque.

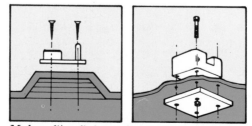

Make a firm fixing point for fittings.

Bolts and Machine Screws Whe bolting is recommended for a fitting machine screws, which are available i brass and stainless steel, can be used They are cheaper than bolts, the head can be countersunk and they can be cu to length. Shorten by threading the nu onto the screw and using a hacksaw File off burrs and unscrew the nu Hexagonal headed bolts are best fo pivots on centreboards and rudder because of their smooth bearin surface. On rudder pivot bolts use nail punch to rivet on the nut and t prevent it unthreading. Always bac the nut with a suitable washer.

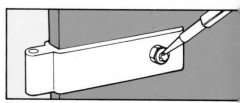

Rivet nut on rudder pivots.

Wood Screws are available with a number of head recesses, the slotted head being the most common. To prevent splitting the timber or breaking the screw, counterbore a suitable hole. Then drill a larger hole to accept the shank, wrapping a small piece of tape around the drill bit to show the depth required. If necessary, allow for the head of the screw to be countersunk. With screws that require periodic tightening and large screws, smear the threads first with grease to prevent breakages when tightening. Too much grease will stain the wood or prevent the glue from adhering. The table below shows the size of hole required for different gauges of screw:

Screw Gauge	Drill Size for Shank	Counter-bore	Counter-sink
4	$^{3}/_{32}$ (2.5)	gimlet	$^{1}/_{4}$ (6)
6	$^{5}/_{32}$ (3.5)	$^{1}/_{16}$ (1.5)	$^{5}/_{16}$ (8)
8	$^{3}/_{16}$ (4.5)	$^{3}/_{32}$ (2.5)	$^{3}/_{8}$ (9)
10	$^{13}/_{64}$ (5)	$^{1}/_{8}$ (3)	$^{7}/_{16}$ (11)
12	$^{1}/_{4}$ (6)	$^{1}/_{8}$ (3)	$^{1}/_{2}$ (12)

Self Tapping Screws are only available in stainless steel. Drill holes slightly larger than the shank so that the thread can cut a groove into the GRP or aluminium. When fixing to a GRP hull, apply a mastic tape between the fitting and the skin to seal the screw holes and to remove unevenness in the fitting. The size of the screw holes should be as follows:

Screw Gauge	Hole Size
6	$^{3}/_{32}$ (2.5)
8	$^{7}/_{64}$ (3)
10	$^{1}/_{8}$ (3)

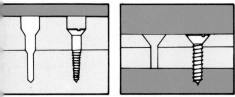

Slot screw holes: wood, self tapping.

Barbed Ring Nails have similar holding powers to screws but are cheaper and lighter. However, once driven home they cannot be easily removed. Choose silicone bronze nails. For larger nails drill pilot holes half the diameter of the nail.

Pop Rivets are used for trims on GRP hulls and on metal spars. Use only monel rivets. If possible buy blind rivets, otherwise fill open ones with a plastic plug. Drill holes with a clearance drill bit. Always apply a zinc chromate paste to the back of stainless steel fittings before fixing to metal masts.

Copper Boat Nails rely considerably on the glue join, as they do not have strong holding power. Two pieces of plywood can be glued and held together by clenching the copper nails over to form a rivet. Drill pilot holes half the thickness of the diagonal on hard wood.

Brass Panel Pins should be driven home and punched below the surface. Varnish over and then fill. Space pins neatly.

Barbed ring nail.

Copper boat nail.

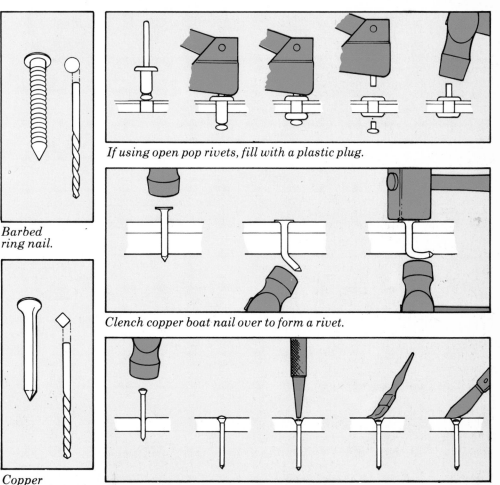

If using open pop rivets, fill with a plastic plug.

Clench copper boat nail over to form a rivet.

Space brass panel pins neatly using dividers.

GLUES

Synthetic resin glues are used for joining wood to wood, for example for joints, repairs or patches, and when fixing stiffening battens. Alternatively you can use epoxy. For joining wood to GRP or GRP to GRP, use resin and tape or an epoxy adhesive (see Index).

Glues must be water resistant and capable of filling a gap of 0.05" (1.3 mm) There are three types of wood glue. All are cured using a catalyst or hardener.

Urea-Formaldehyde Glue This is the most popular. It is reasonably cheap and ideal for use where the timbers are fastened with nails or screws in addition to the glue. You can either buy it pre-mixed, or the glue and hardener separately. In this case the hardener is applied separately. Both types come in powder form and are mixed with water to make liquid glue. In its powder state the glue has a shelf life of about two years. Once mixed with water, the separate application glue will last up to three months, but the pre-mixed type must be used immediately. With the pre-mixed glue apply glue to one surface only. With the separate application glue apply a thin film evenly over one of the surfaces, and apply hardener to the other surface just prior to bringing the two surfaces together. Too much hardener will seep through the screw or nail holes and cause staining. Bring the two surfaces together quickly and apply pressure.

Phenol and Resorcinal Glues These glues should be used where the join relies completely on the glue, for example planking on clinker built hulls. They are mixed with a catalyst which begins to cure immediately, so only mix the quantity required. Apply to one surface only. Being coloured they will stain, so keep the work clean and remove any excess as soon as possible. Their shelf life is 6-9 months.

1. Use pre-mixed glue on a small repair.
2. Using hardener separately.

General Applications The wood t be glued must always be dry and free paint or other materials. The moistu content of the wood should not excee 20%. Oily timbers such as Guarea a difficult to glue, although har sanding of the surfaces immediatel prior to application will help. Th temperature of the workshop extremely important, so keep constant heat while curing glues. A 50°F (10°C) the cure time is about si hours; at 68°F (20°C) it is about tw hours. A light bulb placed under th boat will provide an adequate source heat. Store powders in a dry cool plac and never allow glues to freeze.

If you are going to use screws, dri holes for these before gluing, counte sinking if necessary. Mark out the glu areas carefully in advance, makin sure that the panels will fit. O plywood and small timbers, sand th surfaces to be glued with 60 grit pap across the grain. On larger areas suc as scarfs or laminates, score th surfaces diagonally with a saw chisel for better adhesion. Remove an bumps or wood fibres that coul prevent a good bond.

Apply glue with a flat stick spreading evenly over the whol surface. Too little glue will caus failure of the join, but too much wi ooze out of the join as soon as you appl pressure. If the hardener is applie separately, spread it on using a stic with a piece of cloth wrapped aroun one end. Apply pressure by screwin nailing or cramping. When crampin place pieces of scrap timber under th shoes of the cramp to prever damaging the work. If excess glue likely to come into contact with th timber, cover the join with greaseproo paper first. Apply even pressure acros the whole of the join, using if necessar a stout piece of timber to span the joi then cramp. Remove excess glue with damp cloth immediately after applyin pressure, or remove with a chisel whe it has gelled. Clean the chisel. If yo llow the excess to harden, it will be ifficult to remove and you could amage the wood in the process. Leave ne work undisturbed for at least six hours, or twelve if the join relies solely on the glue. The bond will take about ten days to achieve full strength.

When laminating rudder blades or centreboards using synthetic glues, do not rely solely on the glue join. Dowell the timbers. These wooden pins will prevent the joins from splitting.

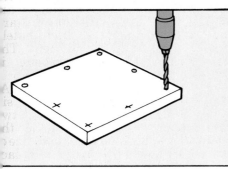

rill screw holes before gluing.

Mark out gluing area in advance.

Always make sure that panels fit.

and small surfaces with 60 grit paper.

Score larger surfaces with saw or chisel.

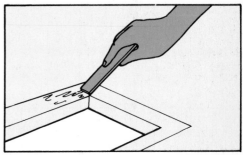

Spread glue evenly over the surface.

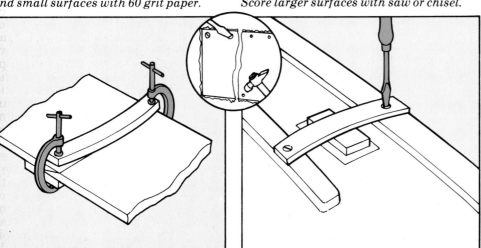

pply even pressure until the glue sets, and wipe off excess glue as soon as possible.

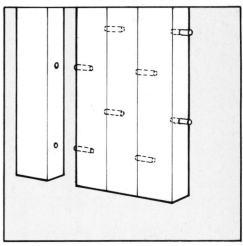

Dowell timbers on laminated foils.

EPOXY SYSTEMS

There are many epoxy systems on the market, but only two or three are for marine use. The base resin can be used for coating and laminating. When modified with fillers, it becomes an adhesive, whose bonding is far superior to that of synthetic glues and polyester resins. Epoxy systems are expensive, but they enable reductions in fastenings and the quantity of materials and paints normally required.

The first constituent of an epoxy system is the base resin which has to be mixed with hardener. Unlike polyester resins it is essential to achieve the correct proportions. The wrong ratio of hardener will result in a weaker cure. Use a ratio of five parts resin to one part hardener. In order to achieve the correct ratio it is advisable to buy the special syringes or pumps available. The resin cures quickly, so mix only small quantities at a time. When using as a coating, mix the resin in a plastic tray and apply with a disposable sponge roller.

The resin must be applied in warm and dry conditions. In a cold damp atmosphere the amine hardener will pick up moisture from the air, and this will show as a cloudy film in the cured material. The ideal temperature is between 61° F (16° C) and 77° F (25° C).

The base resin makes an excellent coating for wooden boats, as it both penetrates and strengthens the timber as well as keeping out all moisture. Apply three coats. Apply the next coat as soon as the previous one is touch dry. If allowed to harden, dry sand with 220 grit between coats. After the final coats sand wet and dry with 400 grit. Finish with a coat of two part polyurethane paint or varnish to protect the resin from ultra violet light. As an alternative to the base resin, there is an epoxy resin which has been developed for coating only. This is two parts resin to one part hardener, and because it contains solvent it is lighter than the base resin. It achieves a much higher build than other paint systems.

A further advantage of epoxy coating is that materials can be coated prior to assembly and bonding with epoxy adhesive.

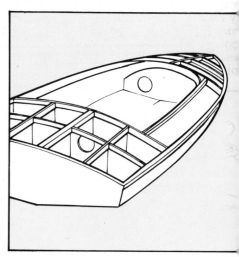
Coating before assembly.

The base resin can also be used as an alternative to polyester resin to laminate glass tape and for the other laminating jobs described in this book. If applying to vertical surfaces, add a small proportion (4%) of coloidal silica to the resin to prevent sagging.

Equipment.

Coating with roller.

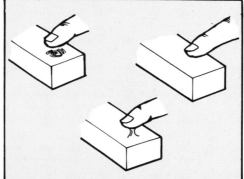
Testing for touch dry.

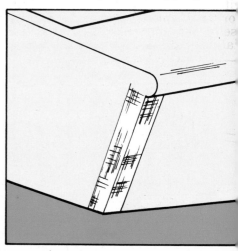
When laminating, prevent slips.

In order to create an epoxy adhesive dd coloidal silica to the consistency of thick syrup. Apply to one surface nly. Where the join is not a perfect fit r there is a fair sized gap, make a filler y adding more silica to the mix. This hicker mix is also ideal for filling deep cores and cracks on all boats. It is escribed elsewhere in the book as olventless epoxy filler. It can be

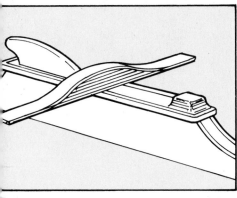

sing as adhesive on centrecases.

pplied to bare wood or glassfibre, and lso to two part polyurethane painted urfaces. It does not adhere well to onventional painted surfaces. This ller does not shrink, so finish flush ith the surface and only sand lightly. or small emergency repairs you can se epoxy adhesive available commer-ially.

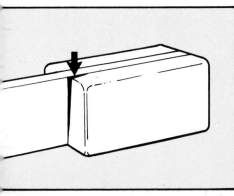

sing as filler on large gaps.

To join two panels (a 'T' join) use an epoxy fillet. This strong but light-weight join takes the place of a wood batten or a tape join. Add inorganic microspheres or microballoons to the thick glue mix and apply the fillet each side of the join. Fillets are normally $\frac{5}{8}''$ (16 mm) wide, or if extra strength is required $\frac{3}{4}''$ (20 mm) wide. Spoon the mixture onto the join with a spatula or plastic disc. Draw the spatula or disc along the join pressing the epoxy well in. The resultant fillet once cured will be stronger than the material it is bonding, so only minimal fastenings need hold it in position while the epoxy hardens.

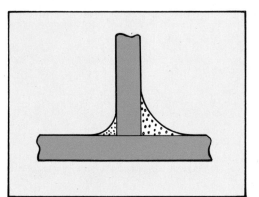

Types of fillet.

Mixing for a fillet.

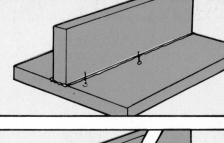

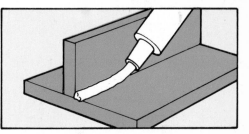
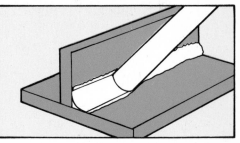
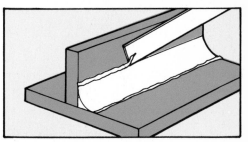

Making an epoxy fillet on a T join.

GENERAL REMARKS

When you get the boat home decide how much work has to be done. Plan the best order to work so that you waste no time. Make a list of all jobs to be done and materials required. Always work under cover.

Paints and varnishes are available in two systems, the conventional system (alkyd type paints and one can polyurethanes) and the two part polyurethane system. These can be used on all types of boat. Remember to use the correct solvent for your system. Although varnishes are less durable than paints and require more coats to achieve the same thickness, they enhance the colouring and patterns of natural timbers. Use on strategic points such as the floor, centrecase and transom so that you can spot any problems. Apply a minimum of four coats.

Make sure that you use the right system for your boat, as it is not advisable to change. However carefully you strip the hull, there is bound to be some old paint left on the surface which will prevent a new system bonding properly. Nor should you use

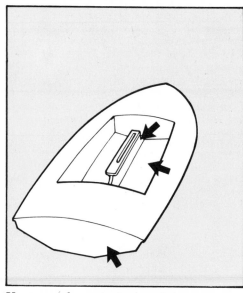

Use varnish on strategic points.

one system on the outside of the boat and another on the inside. As moisture can enter the surface through conventional coatings, it could become trapped under a two part polyurethane system on the other side.

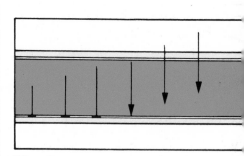

What happens if you combine systems.

Start by washing off all dirt and grease from the boat, and on GRP remove any polish with acetone followed by sandpaper. Go over the boat carefully to see that the materials are sound, and check all parts and fittings. You should carry out all repairs and deal with all problems prior to coating. Careful preparation of the surface avoids most painting problems. Imperfections will always show through the top coat. If any parts of the boat are saturated, leave to dry out properly.

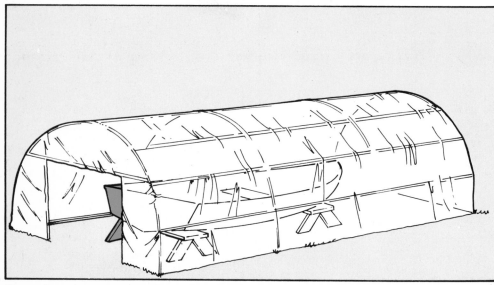

To work under cover you can erect a temporary greenhouse.

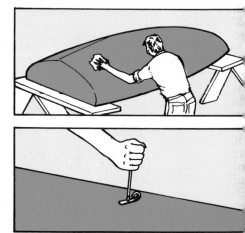

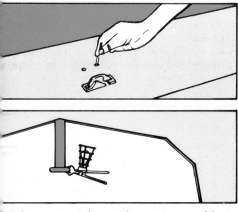

Good preparation avoids coating problems.

Preparing GRP hull for painting.

Wooden boats normally require a new coat of paint or varnish each year. Decide how much stripping to do. Only in very bad cases is it necessary to go back to bare wood. Just go back to a sound surface. Remove defective material, such as flaking, peeling or bubbling paint or varnish, as described later in this section. On patches where you need to go back to bare wood follow the coating instructions below for your system. On patches where only the surface has broken down, sand the area feathering back the old material, and build up with the correct coating until you reach the thickness of the rest of the hull coat. Prepare the complete hull for coating by sanding dry with 220 grit. Follow the instructions in this section for cleaning and coating.

On GRP boats you can use any type of paint system, but it is recommended to cover the gel coat, even on a new boat, with a two part polyurethane. This is because it is more water resistant than gel coat. If coating GRP for the first time, abrade the surface with 220 grit. If removing old paint, sand as described. Do not strip paint unless necessary. Prepare the complete hull for coating by sanding dry with 220 grit. Follow the instructions in this section for cleaning, filling and coating. Whichever system you use, apply a glassfibre primer.

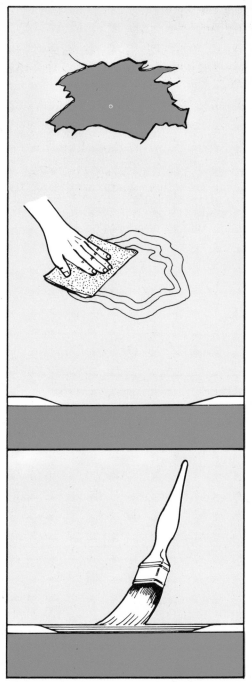

Feather back coated edge and build up.

When buying fillers, make sure that the material will be compatible with your paint system. For the correct time to apply filler when coating, refer to the instructions for your system. Do not use filler on a poor glue join. Instead use epoxy (*see* **Fastenings**) or mix sawdust with waterproof wood glue. Too much stopping will trap solvents and increase shrinkage.

There are various special paints you might need to use. Bilge paints are an alkyd type of paint designed for larger boats. Use for interiors of buoyancy tanks in wooden boats, and apply over primer. Anti-fouling paints are recommended if the boat is kept on a mooring. Apply to areas beneath the waterline. They are very toxic, so follow instructions carefully. Non-slip paints have a rough matt finish and are for use on floors, and also on the decks of trapeze boats.

Check that you have all the necessary tools for stripping, filling and coating. Keep them clean and sharp. Here is a list:
Scrapers
Paint Removers
Sandpaper (60, 100, 150, 220, 400, 600 grit)
Brushes and Paint Pads
Fillers and Filling Tools
Paints, Varnishes, Solvents
Rags, Tacky Cloth
Masking Tape

PAINT REMOVING

When going back to bare wood you can remove paint by burning off, using a chemical remover or scraping and sanding. When going back to a sound surface or on GRP, sand only.

Burning Off Use a propane gas blow lamp or hot air stripper. The hot air stripper has the advantage of not producing a flame liable to char the wood. Do not use these on GRP because glassfibre is inflammable. Varnish should only be burned off by an expert. Do the job with plenty of ventilation. Clear the area of all combustible materials, and check flaming material as it falls to the floor. Heat a small patch of paint and immediately follow the path of the stripper with a hook scraper. Draw the scraper towards you, taking great care not to dig into the corners. Always scrape with the grain. Sand back charred wood with 60 grit paper, and sand the whole hull with 100 and 150 grit.

Stripping old paint with blow lamp.

Chemical Paint Removers normally contain ingredients which can harm glassfibre, so do not use on GRP hulls unless the label specifically states that it is safe to do so. Do not use a remover which is neutralized with water. The quality is inferior. Apply with a brush using a dabbing action, and allow to soak in to the area for ten minutes. Scrape off with a flat scraper, using it in the direction of the grain. The job may require more than one application of remover. Finish up by using the correct agent to neutralize the remover. Take great care to neutralize all the paint especially around any old stoppings. Keep remover off your skin. Have neutralizer handy.

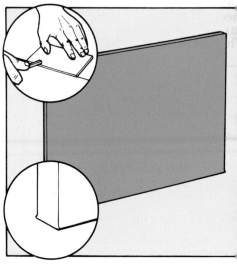

Don't get chemical removers on the skin.

Scrapers Take care not to dig th corners of scrapers into the materia Cabinet scrapers will remove loca areas of paint, varnish or rough grair The bottom edge, which has bee burred over on both sides for cutting requires frequent sharpening. Hol each end of the scraper firmly an press in with the thumbs to form curve in the blade. Holding the blad upright, scrape it across the surface c the work, pushing away from you Paint scrapers will remove paint usin a similar action to stripping wallpape When using a blow lamp, a hoo scraper is best.

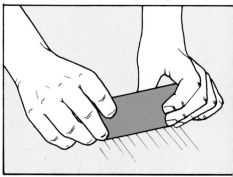

A cabinet scraper. Sharpening (inset).

Using a cabinet scraper.

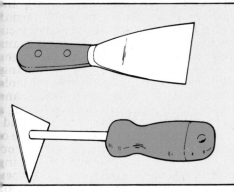

Hook scraper and paint scraper.

Sanding If you are going to use a mechanical sander, never use a disc sander. Only use an orbital sander. This can be used on all surfaces except varnish. If working by hand, on flat even surfaces, wrap paper round a sanding block to obtain even pressure. Always dry sand in the direction of the grain.

On wooden boats go back to bare wood using 60 grit. Smooth the surface with 100 and then 150 grit before coating. On GRP if removing paint going back to bare glassfibre, use 60 grit, taking care not to damage the gel coat. If sanding laminates or filler, it may be necessary to use 50 grit. Finish by preparing the gel coat for painting with 220 grit.

If you are preparing a painted surface for coating on any type of boat, sand with 220 grit.

A liquid sander is also available. Wipe it over the paint, wipe it off again and allow to dry. This flattens the old gloss, and the slightly softened surface will give good adhesion if overcoated within six hours. It may still be necessary to remove imperfections or to feather in the edges of the old paint with sandpaper.

After sanding you must always clean the boat thoroughly before coating. Suck the dust out of the surface with a soft brush fitted to the vacuum cleaner. Otherwise use a dustpan and brush. Finish by wiping over the area once or twice with a cloth soaked in the solvent for your system or with a tacky cloth (a resin impregnated cloth which can be refolded and used several times). Tacky cloths can be bought together with a special bag to keep them in.

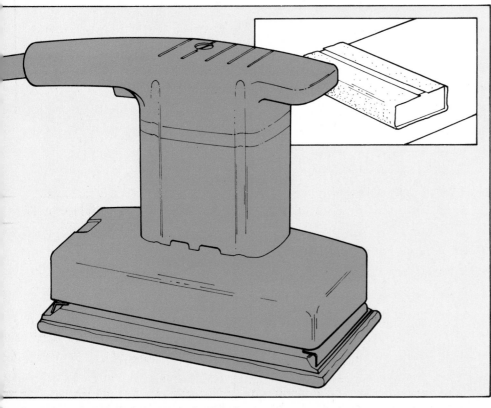

Good sanding techniques improve the finish of coatings.

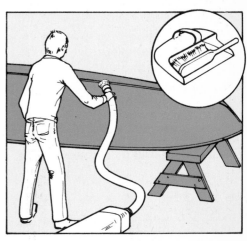

Remove dust from boat before coating.

Finish by using a tacky cloth.

COATING APPLICATIONS

When coating there must be proper ventilation to allow solvents to evaporate and coats to dry. Do not seal up gaps in doors. Cold draughts, however, will cause patchy drying. Do not paint on windy days. Do not paint on wet days either, as water vapour will form a film over the surface and impair adhesion. Coat around midday when the air is driest. Sprinkle water on concrete or dusty floors to lay the dust.

Wear an overall or nylon when coating instead of woollen clothes which will cover the surface with hair and fluff. Work quickly, keeping a wet edge. Joins will be visible if you cannot work fast enough. A wider brush allows more paint to be applied at a time. Never ladle on the paint. If coats are too thick, solvents will be trapped and coatings will remain soft. Follow

The temperature of the workshop is very important. When it is cold, drying and curing will be slow, and when it is too warm materials will be hard to apply. Check the recommended temperature for each product. Under 45° F (7° C) paints and resins will not dry at all. Never add liquid driers, as these will create imbalance in the ingredients. If necessary, heat the workshop before coating and keep warm for 2-3 hours after application. Do not use paraffin heaters, as they give off water vapour.

Do not buy inferior brushes, and look after them well. New brushes will leave bristles behind on the work, so it is better to apply the finishing coat on varnish with a well-kept used brush. Have separate brushes for all finishing coats. Always use the widest practical brush. On the hull exterior use 2½" (65 mm) and 1" (25 mm) around the edges. On the interior or on varnish use a 2" (50 mm) brush and 1" (25 mm) around the edges.

When applying paints and varnishes, dip only the lower third of the brush into the pot. Every 20-30 minutes wipe the excess from the top of the bristles. If using the next day, hang brushes overnight in the correct solvent. If leaving for longer periods, squeeze out excess paint into newspaper, wash bristles several times in solvent, squeeze well and then wash in soapy water. Rinse properly and shake water from the brush. Sponge bristles with an absorbent cloth, smooth them and wrap in foil or cling film. Do not let water or solvent come into contact with brush handles.

A length of wire fixed across the tin to remove excess paint or varnish from brush.

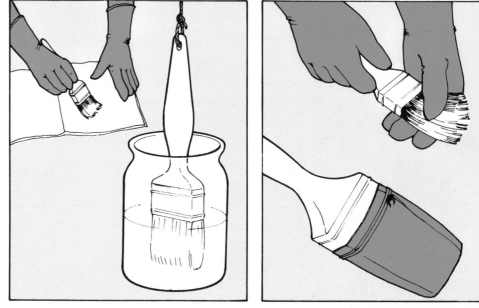

Leaving brushes overnight.

Leaving brushes for longer periods.

he manufacturers' instructions for vercoating times. If a coat is applied oo soon after the last which has not ured properly, solvents will be trapped nd cause bubbling later on. Overoating some polyurethanes after the ecommended expiry time will affect he chemical bond between coats. Sand ry with 220 grit prior to each coat, nd 400 grit prior to the last coat. Clean s described in this section.

If storing an already opened tin, the air trapped inside the tin will cause a skin to form on the surface of the material. To prevent this happening turn the tin upside down for a few minutes when replacing the lid to seal completely. If you use the same tin often for touching up, strain the material free of dust etc with a disposable paint strainer or an old stocking.

Polyurethanes, hardeners and resins contain obnoxious chemicals, so handle carefully. Do not allow contact with skin or eyes. Keep away from children. Resin hardeners can cause severe skin irritation, so use a barrier cream and a gel hand cleaner. Do not clean hands with acetone or solvents. Avoid inhaling fumes. Wear a dust mask when sanding cured paint or resin. Do not put acetone or solvents into plastic containers or handle with plastic gloves. Do not smoke. Read all instructions properly, and wash thoroughly after working.

Names and Waterlines Apply names and initials to sound paint. Use either transfers which should be coated with varnish, or self-adhesive letters. Mark the position with pencil or masking tape. Sign-written names are expensive, but you can make something similar using self-adhesive vinyl. If painting the hull in different colours, on hard chine dinghies use the chine or keel as the dividing lines, and on other boats use the waterline. In the latter case prime the hull first. The waterline is normally the bottom edge of the transom at the centre line. To extend this line, set the boat level 2-3 feet (60-100 cm) off a flat floor. Check the levelness of the boat by plumbing the top of the centrecase and/or mast step horizontal and the transom vertical. Place a batten across the gunwales to check that they are horizontal. Make up a T square on a stand to the height of the waterline off the floor. Move this around the boat marking the hull every 18-24″ (50-60 cm) including the widest point of the boat. Join up these marks with masking tape. Check the line by eye. Turn the boat over and apply paint to first area up to masking tape. Remove tape after sufficient coats. Apply fresh masking tape to new hardened paint, and keeping the same line paint the second area. Self-adhesive vinyl stripes can be applied to sound paint, parallel to the gunwale about 3″ (75 mm) below it.

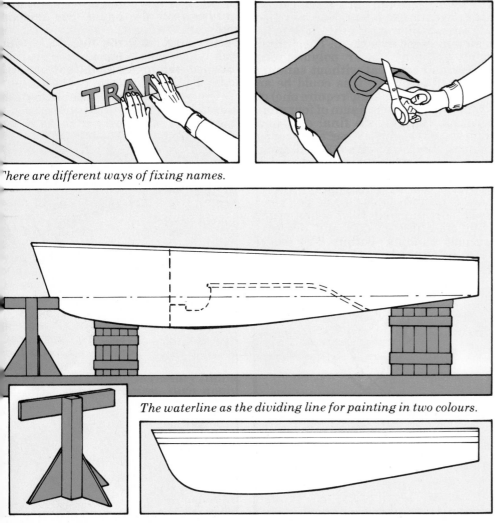

There are different ways of fixing names.

The waterline as the dividing line for painting in two colours.

A T square.

Apply self adhesive vinyl stripes to sound paint only.

RESINS AND GLASSFIBRE MATERIALS

For all practical purposes you will require two types of resin: a gel coat resin and a standard polyester resin. It is best to buy these at boat shops, otherwise always state that the polyester resin is required for use on contact mouldings. Some resins are more impervious to water and weathering than others, so it is important to obtain the correct one. Specific applications are described elsewhere (*see* Index).

Resins are mixed with a catalyst. Buy catalyst at the same time as the resin to ensure that it is the right one. Before mixing allow resins to reach workshop temperature, and have all materials such as mat or tape ready cut to the required size. The curing time of resins is determined by temperature and the amount of catalyst used. Follow the instructions on the container for the correct mixing proportions. The average resin requires 1-2% of catalyst. An easy way to measure the right ratio is one teaspoon of catalyst to $\frac{1}{2}$ pint (250 ml) resin. At 65°F (18°C) a 1% mix will cure in about 40 minutes, while a 2% mix at the same temperature will cure in about 20 minutes. Lower temperatures extend curing time and higher temperatures reduce it. Do not use resins when it is under 59°F (15°C). Mix the catalyst thoroughly into the resin to obtain an even cure, and do not mix more than you can use before it hardens. Store resins in a cool dry place out of sunlight, and remember they are inflammable. Their shelf life is three to nine months.

Gel Coat Resin The exterior surface of the GRP hull is coated with a layer of gel coat resin. This is both more water resistant and more abrasion resistant than ordinary resin. It is also more flexible. Ordinary resin will crack up unless it is strengthened with synthetic fibres in order to create the laminates of the hull. Use gel coat resin for touching up and repairs. For small jobs you can buy it in paste form. Do not mix the pigments yourself, as they are very toxic, and it is difficult to disperse the pigments evenly into the resins. Clean GRP hulls regularly with liquid detergent. Avoid abrasive cleaners, as they will scratch the surface. To achieve a good finish burnish the gel coat with 600 grit paper, wet, apply a rubbing compound and then polish with wax. Do not use silicone polish, as this is hard to remove. The application of a two part polyurethane paint system over the gel coat will increase water resistance and improve the appearance of the GRP hull.

Polish gel coat resin.

Standard Polyester Resin is used for laminating, taping and sealing the edges on repairs. It is used in conjunction with mat to repair holes. Apply with a brush.

Apply release agent.

Paint on gel coat.

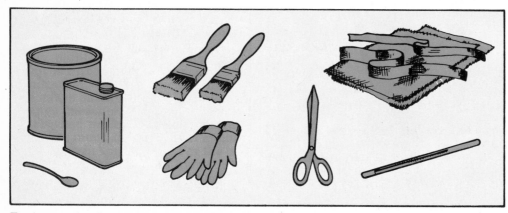
Equipment for the use of resins. Remember the gloves.

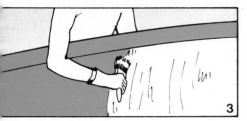

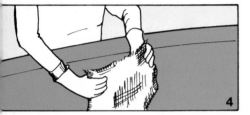

Apply lay up resin.

Apply glassfibre material.

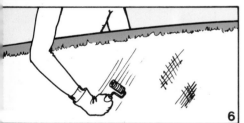

Stipple down with brush.

Consolidate with roller.

Apply next layer, and repeat 5. and 6.

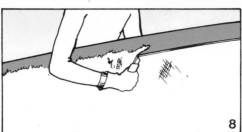

Trim off rough edges.

Chopped Strand Mat is made from strands of glass particles matted together with an emulsion. It is a general material for making laminates and is available in different strengths, the common one for boats being $450\,g/m^2$.

Glassfibre Fabric is stronger than chopped strand mat. It is used where a thin laminate with a good surface finish is required, or for reinforcing. For example, it makes a good shape round large curves. It is a wide tape available in open or close weave. The open weave (scrim) offers greater strength and better adhesion.

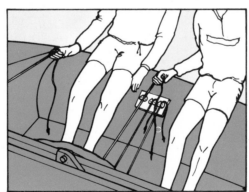

Glassfibre fabric for curved areas.

Polyester Body Filler should only be used in small doses on GRP hulls. Apply a resin over it to make it water resistant. You can make it by mixing talc into polyester resin, or you can buy it ready-mixed.

Glassfibre Tape is used with polyester or epoxy resin for repairs and bonding seams on all types of boat.

Epoxy Resin The base resin is an excellent coating for wooden boats and parts. It can also be used for laminating instead of polyester resin. If modified with fillers, it becomes an excellent adhesive (*see* **Fastenings**).

Surfacing Tissue is a very fine mat which can be used to cover cracks on wooden hulls. It is also used as a backing to the gel coat prior to laminating to strengthen or reduce the thickness of the gel coat. Apply as for taping.

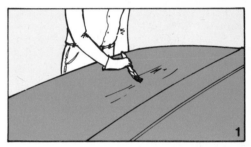

Paint on gel coat.

Apply surfacing tissue.

Apply lay up resin.

GENERAL PRINCIPLES

Most repairs are within the capabilities of the average handyman. Insurance firms often encourage home repairs.

Before attempting any repairs care must be taken in the preparation of the damaged areas. Cut back to sound material, although on scores and cracks this should be kept to a minimum. Wash the area to remove all traces of salt and grease. Remove dust with a vacuum cleaner and brush.

Abrade surfaces onto which glue or resin is to be applied. Glues and resins will not adhere properly to painted or polished surfaces. You should follow the manufacturer's instructions when preparing resins (*see* **Coatings and Finishes**) and mix thoroughly. A total cure is often not affected due to the catalyst being unevenly mixed into the resin. Do not apply glues, resins or paints to wet or damp surfaces.

Work in a well-ventilated area. Do not smoke or inhale the fumes when mixing or using chemicals. Follow the recommended instructions for mixing, using and safety for each chemical. Make sure that a colleague or member of the family knows what to do in the event of an accident. Keep all chemicals out of the reach of children.

Always wipe GRP boats with acetone prior to applying coats of resin. Beware of allowing acetone to remain on the gel coat, as prolonged contact will damage the glassfibre. Allow it to evaporate, and do not trap under fresh resin.

Besides the conventional forms of heating an electric light bulb will dry out localized areas. If left underneath an upturned boat for a few days it will dry a larger patch. Hair dryers can be used on small patches, and help to disperse air pockets in the fibres. Blow lamps can be used on wood, but not on GRP. Paraffin heaters should be avoided, as they create a damp atmosphere.

Tools In addition to the basic kit the following tools are suggested for the repairs described in this section.
1. Trimming knife to mark out and make clean narrow cuts
2. Back tenon saw to cut small sections of timber
3. Panel saw to cut sheet materials
4. Pad saw to cut holes in panels
5. Firmer chisels: sizes $\frac{1}{4}''$ (6 mm), $\frac{1}{2}''$ (12 mm), $\frac{3}{4}''$ (19 mm) and 1'' (25 mm) to cut and shape materials
6. Mallet to use with chisels
7. Smoothing plane to smooth planed timber and trim panels to size
8. Bull nose plane to smooth rabbets (recesses)
9. Spokeshave to smooth curved or moulded timber
10. Rasp to shape wood and glassfibre in primary stages
11. Sanding block
12. File to clean out grooves and edges of small holes
13. G Cramp to provide pressure while gluing
14. Vice to hold materials firm while working
15. Gimlet to make holes in wood for screws
16. Twist drills, various sizes including a countersink bit
17. Nail punch to drive pins below the surface
18. Try square to square up timber
19. Stopping knife to apply stopper and fillers
20. Roller to consolidate glassfibre laminate
21. Sandpaper: 40 grit on E paper, 60 grit on D paper and 100 grit on C paper

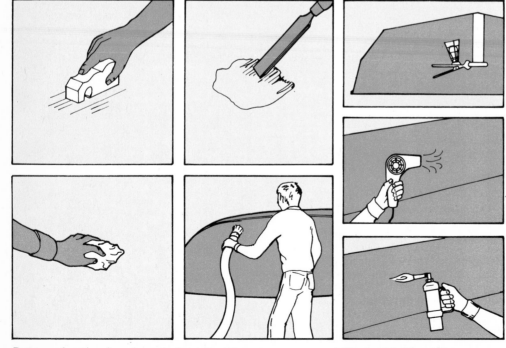

Prepare damaged surfaces before repairing.   *Ways of drying out.*

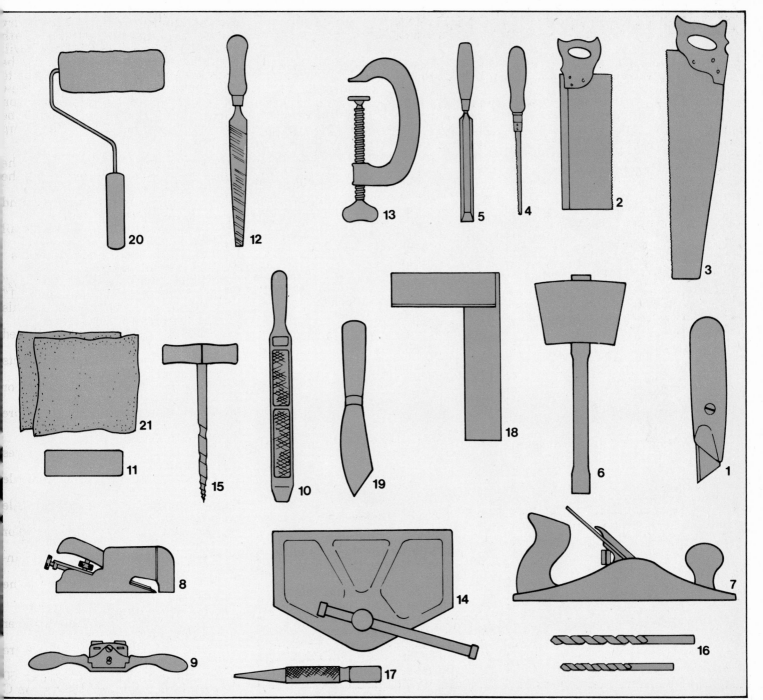

TOOLS AND TECHNIQUES

Before starting work check that you have the necessary tools to hand, and that you know how to use them. Keep tools clean and sharp.

A sharp chisel requires less pressure and cuts better. Start by sawing across the grain at each end of the proposed slot. Chisel from each end towards the centre to reduce the risk of splitting the material. Use a slicing action and finish each cut with an upward movement. Tap with a mallet, never a hammer. Do not use a mallet on GRP.

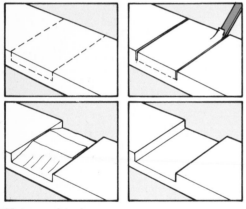

Using a chisel.

When hand paring hold the chisel firmly and work away from yourself. Guide the blade with the finger and thumb of one hand, keeping them well clear of the cutting edge, and apply pressure with the other hand. Do not

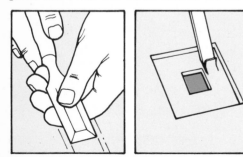

Hand pare following lines of grain.

remove too much waste at a time. If extra pressure is required, use the shoulder. When removing the top veneers of plywood, follow the contour lines of the different veneers for a neat and even finish.

Fairing in is to plane a part of the boat to a similar angle as the adjacent timber so that there are no hard edges. Check constantly with a lath of timber that the line, whether straight or curved, is kept true.

Fairing in to take new panel.

To use the smoothing plane secure the wood in a vice or chock up the boat to prevent movement. Remove nails and screws. Adjust the cutting irons to the correct depth. Do not remove too much waste at a time, and set very fine for removing varnish. Check regularly that the work is square. To prevent dipping apply pressure at the front of the plane when starting each cut and at the back when finishing. Follow the direction of the grain. It helps the slicing action to hold the plane at a

slight angle to the direction of movement. Keep the plane on its side when not in use, and withdraw the cutting iron when storing. Clean regularly during use, and wipe off glue with a damp cloth. Rub the sole with candle wax.

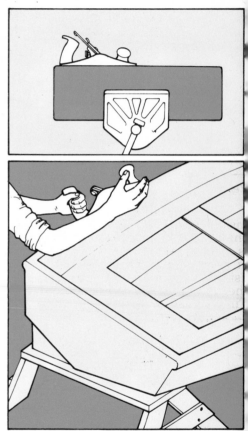

Position the boat at a good working angle.

The spokeshave is ideal for obtaining a rounded narrow section and for blending in edges on small patches or scarf joints. Use like the smoothing plane. When fairing in a curve work from each end into the centre, following the direction of the grain. For splicing in rubbing beads make the curve long and shallow. Finish with sandpaper.

Repairing centreboard with a spokeshave.

The bullnose plane is for smoothing inside rabbets (recesses). Its blade enables it to plane up to a right angle. It is also useful for smoothing the edges of holes. Finish with a chisel. When using a rasp, work from each end into the middle of the wood or laminate. Finish with sandpaper.

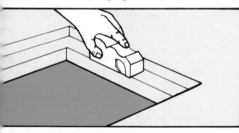

Planing up to a right angle.

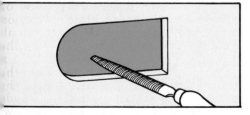

Using a rasp tool.

Chamfering removes the sharp angles at edges by a combination of planing, chiselling and sanding. Feathering takes this a stage further by tapering wood from its true thickness down to nothing over the length of about 2″ (50 mm)

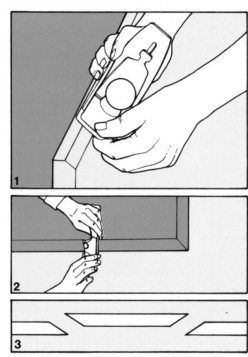

Chamfering (1.). Feathering (2. & 3.).

Scarfing joins two pieces of wood together. With plywood the recommended length of the join is 8:1 (e.g. $\frac{1}{4}$″ (6 mm) ply requires a 2″ (50 mm) join). With timber use 6:1. Plane the two pieces to a feather edge. Pin or cramp the wood to support the feather edge, and plane at an angle to avoid splintering the veneers. The feathering must be uniform across the width of both pieces and the width of each scarf the same on both panels. The panels must be glued together and cramped between two pressure bars. Put grease-proof paper over one bar, apply glue and position the panels. Hammer two

pins through the join into the pressure bar. Cover the join with greaseproof paper, position the second bar and cramp together. Leave for 24 hours. Clean with a spokeshave and sand.

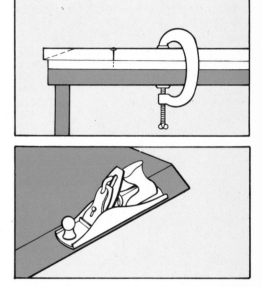

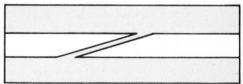

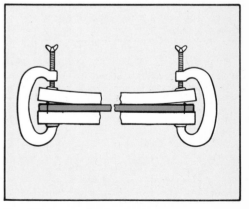

Scarfing procedure.

GLASS TAPE METHODS

Resin and tape is ideal on account of its simplicity and versatility. It bonds and waterproofs a join in one easy operation. You can adapt the applications described below to your own requirements.

The most common sizes of glassfibre tape are 1½″ (38 mm), 2″ (50 mm) and 3″ (75 mm). Of the different constructions available the mock leno type where the weft and warp are locked together does not distort when applying resin. Tape can be used with polyester or epoxy resins. Both types of resin will bond wood or glassfibre. Resin and tape will also bond dissimilar materials such as spinnaker chutes passing through bulkheads.

Apply resin to clean dry surfaces. Remove all paint, polish and release agent. Abrade the surfaces, cut the tape and mix the resin (*see* **Coatings and Finishes**). Mix enough resin for the tape cut. Apply a coat of resin to the seam, slightly wider than the tape. Lay the tape onto the resin, recharge the brush and stipple the tape down. Press it into the corners and flatten. Apply enough resin to soak the tape. Avoid air bubbles by using short brush strokes and working from the centre of the

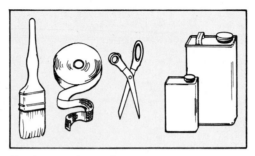

Equipment for taping.

tape. If you find small air bubbles once the resin has cured, drill a hole through the tape and force in more resin. Avoid a large build up of resin. This will cause splits. If the tape distorts, use short strokes or cut darts in the tape. For a thicker consistency, sprinkle a little talc into the resin. Tape sits better on rounded edges than on angles. When the resin has cured and hardened, sand the top surface, remove dust and apply a further coat.

To replace a panel on stitch and glue constructed boats lay the new panel so that it sits on the adjacent one. Drill a series of matching holes in both panels 3″ (75 mm) apart and ⅜″ (9 mm) in from the edge. Thread 2½″ (60 mm) lengths of copper wire through these holes from the inside to join the panels. With pliers twist together the ends of the wire on the outside of the hull. On the inside tap the wire into the configuration of the hull. Apply resin and tape to the inside join. This must cure fully before tackling the outside seam. Cut the wires off flush with the exterior surface with a chisel. Smooth the edge of the panel, slightly rounding the corners. Apply resin and tape to the outside seam.

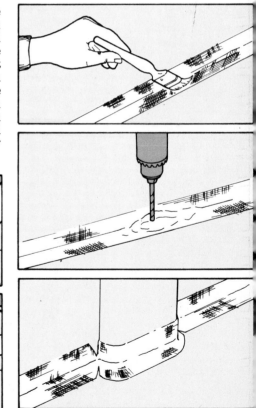

Dealing with problems.

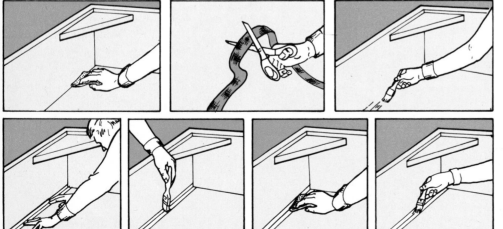

Basic taping method.

On 'T' joins always force the tape into the corners of the seams. First push the stem panel of the inverted 'T' hard down onto the piece to which it must join. Support firmly in position, either from the top or pin and glue to small blocks of wood. Resin and tape both sides of the join.

Flexing of the hull can cause old seams to come away from the wood or glassfibre. Gaps will be seen behind the tape or the tape will turn milky white leaving a water trap. To renew a seam chisel through sound material 2-3" (50-75 mm) each side of the old seam. Use pliers to rip off old tape, pulling at right angles to the join. Sand the surface and chisel away old resin. Apply resin and tape as described.

To fix a reinforcing pad onto glass fibre mark the position of the pad onto the hull. Apply two layers of tape, and press on pad while wet. Tape around the edges and apply pressure until the resin cures. If taping around a fitting block, round off the corners of the block and cut darts in the tape to prevent wrinkling. If covering cracks or strengthening, place two pieces of tape off centre over the crack.

On the hull exterior conceal tape to improve underwater shape. Pare away top veneers to the depth of the tape so that the seam is flush with the rest of the hull. Or apply polyester body filler to smooth the edge of the tape.

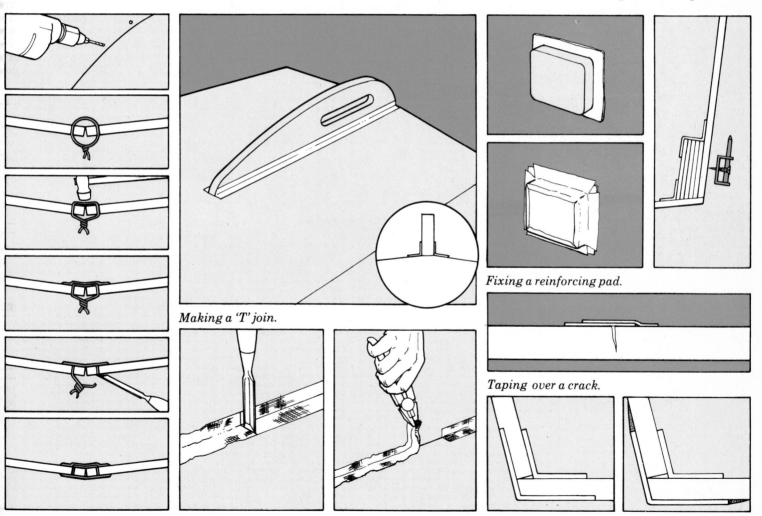

Making a 'T' join.

Fixing a reinforcing pad.

Taping over a crack.

Stitch and glue method.

Renewing an old tape seam.

Hiding tape joins.

PATCHES

If you have a hole in your boat, the type of patch you use will depend on its size and position. If the hole is over 8″ (20 cm) square you may have to replace the whole panel. When buying a secondhand boat, do not be put off by a patch. Just check that the job has been done properly.

When repairing wooden boats remove damaged wood using a pad saw and chisel. Then square out the hole. New wood can be cut to the exact size if the hole is square. Where possible always chamfer or feather the edges in order to give more gluing area.

Veneer Patch This is used for small holes 2-3″ (50-75 mm) square. You will need to cut three patches of wood from a piece of veneer $\frac{1}{16}$″ (1.5 mm) thick. Start by cutting back to sound timber, and square out the hole. On the inside of the hull mark out a square 1″ (25 mm) larger than the hole all round. On the outside mark out a square 2″ (50 mm) larger than the hole. Cut through the outer veneers of the boat with a trimming knife around these marks. Cut the three patches to fit into the two squares you have made and the centre square. Using a sharp chisel pare away the outer veneers within the area of the cuts to the depth required by the three replacement veneers.

Glue the first veneer to the outside of the hull and apply pressure. Glue the next veneer into the centre hole, and glue the final veneer to the inside of the hull. Apply pressure to the whole repair and leave the glue to harden. Trim the patches flush with the skin.

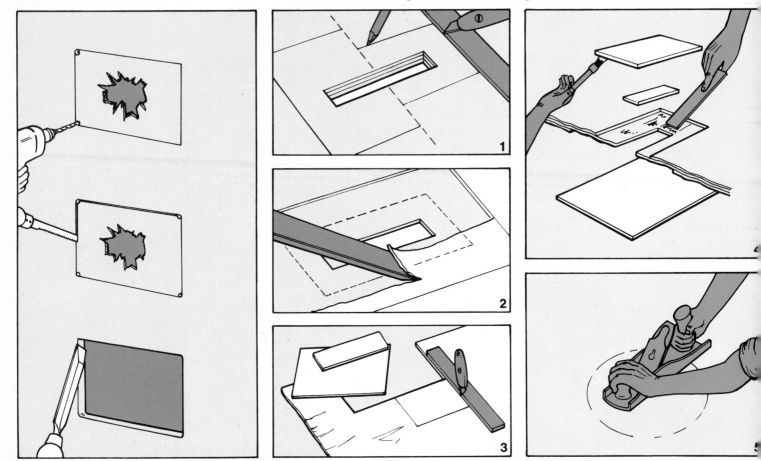

Preparation for all types of patch.

Applying a veneer patch. Complete by trimming with surrounding area.

Scarf Patch This patch is used for holes 4-8″ (10-20 cm) square and should be made from a material of the same thickness and construction as the hull skin. Cut back to sound wood and square out the hole. On the outside of the hull chamfer the edges of the hole to a fine point using both spokeshave and chisel. If the planking is ¼-⅜″ (6-9 mm) thick, make the chamfer at least 2″ (50 mm) wide. Cut the patch to the correct size and chamfer to fit the hole. Fix the patch into place using an epoxy or wood glue. Apply pressure while the glue hardens.

Blind Patch This is used if the hole is accessible from the outside of the hull only. A backing support must be fastened to the inside face. On relatively flat surfaces use ⅜″ (9 mm) plywood for this interior patch. On curved surfaces use 3/16″ (5 mm) plywood.

Cut back to sound material and square out the hole. Cut the inside patch, making it 2″ (50 mm) larger than the hole. On the interior scrape away all traces of paint with coarse sandpaper or a file. Drill a hole through the centre of the inside patch and attach a length of string through it.

Apply glue to the interior of the hull skin. Post the patch through the hole and position it centrally over the hole, holding it in position with the string. Screw through the skin into the patch using ½″ x 6 g brass wood screws. Countersink the heads into the skin.

On GRP complete the repair as described overleaf. On wood cut a second patch the same thickness as the hull skin to fit into the hole. Glue this patch into the hole and screw into place. Wipe off excess glue. When the glue has hardened, fill over the screw heads.

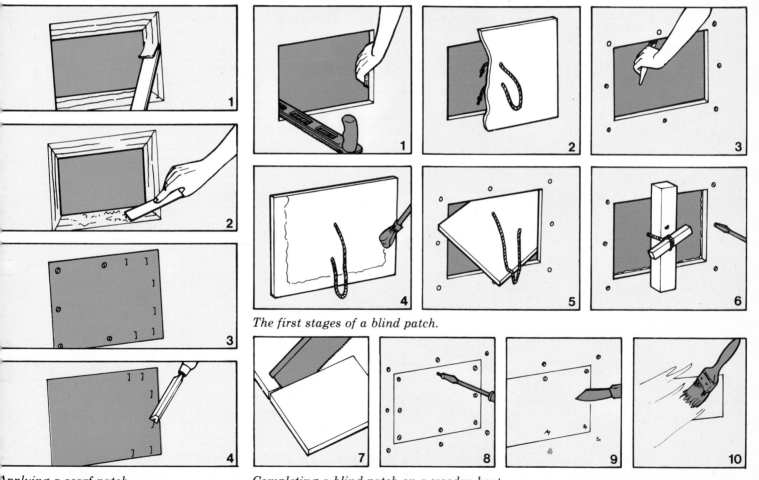

Applying a scarf patch.

The first stages of a blind patch.

Completing a blind patch on a wooden boat.

GRP REPAIRS

Once the gel coat has been scratched away, the exposed glassfibre mat will absorb water. Replace the protective layer immediately.

When cutting glass fibre back to sound material, do so with a sharp chisel and hand pare only. Do not use a mallet, as this could crack the gel coat. Holes do not need to be squared out, but the edges of the hole should be chamfered on both sides to form a 'V' for better adhesion.

Holes Accessible from Both Sides

Cut the damaged area back to sound material and shave inside and outside edges. Wipe with acetone. Tape a piece of cellophane (melinex) covered cardboard to the outside of the hull, completely covering the hole. If the hole is in a curved part of the boat, drill the skin and bolt the cardboard in place. Apply pigmented gel coat resin through the hole onto the back of the covered cardboard. Spread it evenly, and check that air bubbles are not trapped around the edges.

Cut patches of glassfibre mat to the same size as the hole while the gel coat cures. When it is touch dry mix the lay-up resin. Apply a coat of this resin onto the gel coat. Re-charge the brush and stipple in the patches one at a time. Roll out each patch to disperse the trapped air. Build up the repair flush with the inside surface and leave to harden. Remove the cardboard and bolts. Fill the bolt holes with a gel resin putty. Blend the gel coat with the outer surface, and apply a coat of resin over the repair on the inside of the hull.

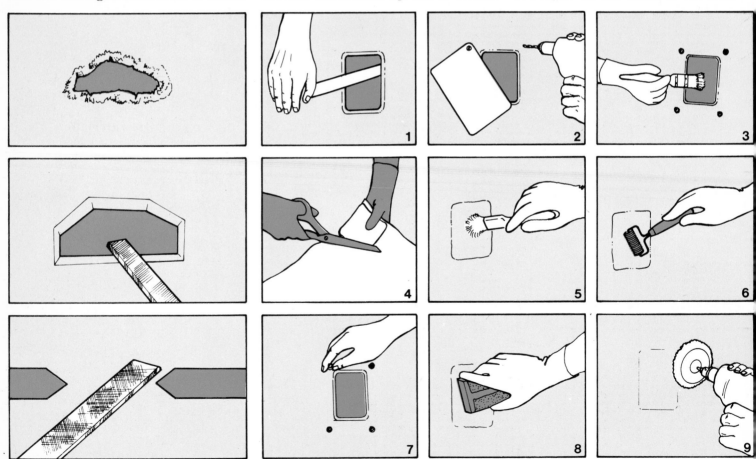

Preparation for all types of repair.

Patching holes which are accessible from both sides of the boat.

Holes Accessible from the Outside Only

Cut the hole back to sound material and wipe over with acetone. This repair requires a patch on the inside of the skin. If the damage is on a straight surface, apply a ⅜″ (9 mm) plywood patch as described for a Blind Patch on the previous page. Treat the skin with resin before fixing.

If the damage is on a curved surface, apply a laminated glassfibre patch. Mark the outline of the hole onto a perforated zinc plate available from glassfibre merchants. Allow for an overlap of 2″ (50 mm) all around the hole and cut the plate to the required shape. Use the zinc plate to cut five layers of glassfibre mat to the same shape. Saturate the zinc plate with resin on a worktop protected with plastic. Stipple on the first piece of mat with more resin. Roll it out with short strokes to remove air bubbles. Repeat with four more pieces of mat. The wet laminations must be positioned at the back of the hole before the resin begins to harden. Pierce both ends of a piece of wire through the mesh and laminate. Press the laminate back down around the wires. You may need two or more lengths of wire depending on the size of the hole. Fold the plate and laminate and push through the hole. Draw it into position by pulling on the wires. Twist the wires around a batten held away from the hull with spacing blocks, and hold the laminate securely in place. When the resin has hardened remove the batten and wires.

To complete both types of repair mix resin with filler powder and build up the hole so that it is just proud of the surface. On a vertical plane make the mix as stiff as possible. When the filler is hard sand down to the profile of the hull. Apply a coat of pigmented gel coat resin and blend with the surrounding surface.

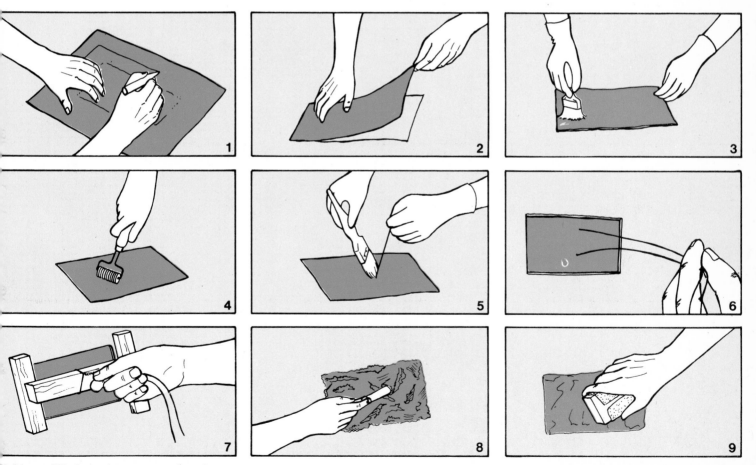

Making a blind patch on a curved surface.

85

CRACKS, SCORES, RUBBING BEADS

On wooden boats cracks are treated differently depending on whether they are in high stress areas on the hull or in low stress areas on the side. On GRP there is no such distinction. Wooden rubbing beads are fitted to most types of boat. If damaged, repair quickly.

Cracks and Scores on GRP Treatment of cracks is described elsewhere in this book (*see* **Hull Care and Maintenance**). With scores start by cleaning and removing all traces of polish from around the damaged area. Dry and wipe over with acetone. Sand the groove with 220 grit paper, and fill with a solventless epoxy filler. Build up to just below the surface. Top up with gel coat resin. Knife the resin in taking care not to trap air bubbles under the coating. Prevent the gel resin from sliding out by taping a piece of cellophane over the repair. The smoother and tighter the cellophane, the neater the finish on the gel coat. When the resin has cured, sand with 400 and 600 grit, wet. Finish off by using a cutting compound.

Cracks in Low Stress Areas and Shallow Scores Open the crack and force wood glue into it. Allow to dry. On the outside of the hull saw or scratch a shallow groove along the line of the crack. Clean out the score with coarse sandpaper or file. Remove loose or splintered wood. Using glue and sawdust build up the groove onto the untreated timber slightly proud of the adjacent surface. Sand flush with the hull panel and paint.

Cracks in High Stress Areas and Multiple Scores Take a piece of veneer about $\frac{1}{16}''$ (1.5 mm) thick. Cut two steps out of the boat timber following the line of the crack if applicable, each to the thickness of the veneer. The deepest cavity should be 1" (25 mm) wider than the crack, and the second 2" (50 mm) wider. Open up the crack and squeeze in wood glue. Cut the

veneer to size and glue into the cavitie Apply pressure or staple (with bras pins or office stapler) until the glue ha hardened. Trim the patch flush wit the surrounding skin, and fill aroun the veneer as necessary. Sand an paint.

Deep Scores Chisel and saw uniform groove along the score. Glue a sliver of timber or fill with solventless epoxy filler. For this repa it is important to use the best filler.

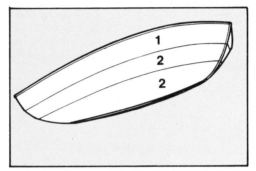
High (1.) and low (2.) stress areas.

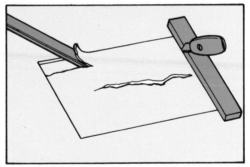
High stress areas: cut the outer veneer.

Cut and chisel out inner veneer.

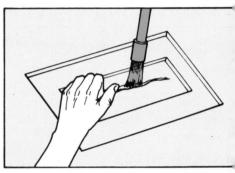
Force glue into crack. Cut new veneers.

Glue in veneers. Tack with staples.

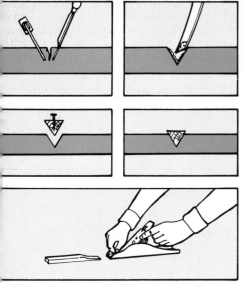

Use the best filler on deep scores.

Rubbing Beads On minor abrasions scrape off the damaged wood with a spokeshave, finishing up with a fair curve. Shape a piece of mahogany to a similar curve and glue it in position. When the glue has hardened plane down the new timber to the correct profile.

When a short length of beading needs replacing, saw through the rubbing bead 4″ (10 cm) either side of the damage. Cut diagonally so that the timber can be scarfed at each end. Remove the fixing, and chisel the timber away carefully exposing the side of the boat. Clean the gunwale line and remove old glue or mastic. Cut a new piece of mahogany to the correct length, and shape the ends as required for the scarf. Use the same type of fixings as on the original beading, but do not use the same fixing holes. Glue must be applied to the ends of the mahogany where they are scarfed onto the original beading. To fasten the wood to the boat surface, on wood use glue and on GRP use mastic. Smooth the new piece flush with the old piece and varnish.

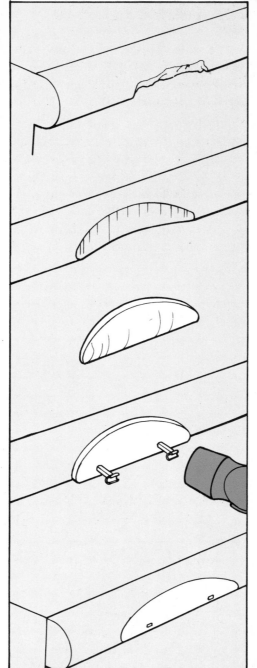

Rubbing beads: repairing minor abrasions.

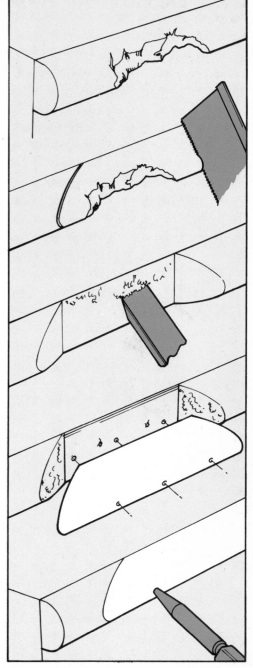

Rubbing beads: replacing a short piece.

TYPES OF PROBLEMS

Faults on dinghies appear only minor at first. It is only when they are not dealt with that they become problems. The main causes of problems are described overleaf. Use the index for guidance on remedies.

GRP

Fine Cracks will appear in the gel coat, mainly on unsupported panels or as hinge cracks along longitudinal joints. Cause: flexing, impact damage. Remedy: reinforce as necessary, then touch up with gel coat and burnish.

Deep Cracks and Splits are usually star shaped. They will have penetrated the gel coat revealing fibrous material. Cause: fine cracks which have not been dealt with, impact damage, hard spots. Remedy: reinforce the laminate, open up the cracks, dry out. Repair cracks with epoxy filler and restore gel coat.

Split Seams are separated joins between panels such as between side-tanks and floor, decking and hull, or timber fitting pads and hull. Cause: flexing, impact damage, ageing. Remedy: remove old resin and tape, repair cracks or holes, fix supports to panels if necessary, replace pads, apply new resin and tape.

Chipping is when small areas of gel coat have broken away from the laminations. Cause: flexing, impact damage, ageing, excessive wear. Remedy: dry out area completely, fill dents and waterproof with gel coat resin or a paint system.

Blisters and Pitting occur in the gel coat, and some blisters burst to form a series of cavities. Cause: osmosis, wicking. Remedy: cut out blister with chisel or knife and dry thoroughly. On large areas remove whole portions of gel coat by abrading with an orbital sander, then strip with a hot air heat gun or by sand blasting. Dry out the hull completely. If boats are kept on moorings, treat the area below the waterline with an epoxide resin system, followed by anti-fouling paint. On most dinghies and above the waterline use two part polyurethane. Dry out the exposed laminate and seal with two coats of the right system and overcoat. If very large areas are affected, consult a professional.

Delamination is shown as water sodden bulges in the gel coat, which will be flexible when touched. Cause: laminations not wetted out properly during construction, frost. Remedy: cut away as much as possible of the affected area. Saturate the edges of the surface with resin to fill any cavities of dry laminate which may still be apparent. Repair hole. If large areas are affected, consult a professional.

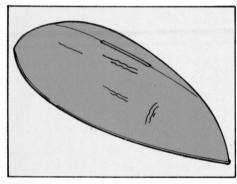
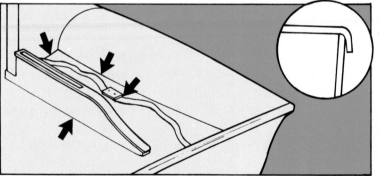

Fine cracks on unsupported panels.   *Check for split seams. Deck panel (inset).*   *Blisters.*

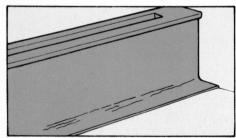
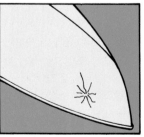
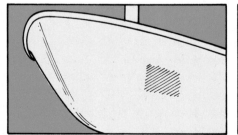

Hinge cracks along the centrecase.   *Star cracks.*   *Delamination: it is important to soak edges with resin.*

WOOD

Cracks or Crazing of the paint or varnish are caused by flexing, impact damage or weathering. Remedy: remove coating with a cabinet scraper, not sanding, to check that timber is unaffected. Reinforce if necessary with extra stiffeners or battens, prime to waterproof timber and build up as required. Persistant cracking of plywood requires stronger measures such as coating with epoxy or laminating a surfacing tissue.

Large Cracks usually affect more than one lamination of plywood or show splits in solid timber. Cause: flexing, impact damage, weathering. Remedy: apply a veneer patch, stiffen with a batten if necessary to prevent further cracking, then finish the repair using paint or varnish.

Black Stains and swelling of wood are the first visible signs of rot. Cause: weathering, untreated cracks, trapped water, broken glue joins. Remedy: remove varnish, bleach out bad stains with a proprietary colour restorer or oxalic acid. This is poisonous. Mix acid to a weak solution with water and start by applying this only to a small experimental patch. You may need two applications. Neutralize with water. Wash carefully with water, dry, sand, prime. If staining occurs near buoyancy tanks, you should fit more ventilation.

Wet Rot means that wood is soft and swollen, and coatings will not adhere. Cause: poor maintenance, trapped water. Remedy: remove coating, dry, cut back to sound wood, repair as appropriate, prime.

Blisters in the coating indicate an incompatible paint system, presence of moisture or contamination of surface prior to coating. Remedy: scrape away sample of coating to check that wood is unaffected. Strip affected area as far as necessary. Dry, sand, wash down with solvent to remove contamination, then re-coat.

Bubbles in plywood appear as a flexible dome in the outer veneer. Cause: lack of glue between veneers. Remedy: cut a cross into bubble with sharp blade, dry cavity with hair dryer. Peel back veneers carefully and force epoxy adhesive or wood glue into the cross. Remove excess, cover with greaseproof paper and apply pressure.

Stiffening batten. Screw if possible.

A surfacing tissue on persistant cracks.

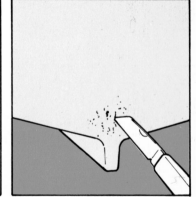

Remove rotten wood.

Bubbles: cut cross.

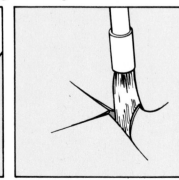

Peel back veneer.

Force in glue.

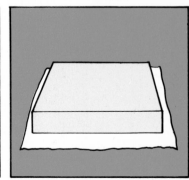

Apply pressure.

CAUSES OF PROBLEMS

In order to be able to identify the specific problems described on the previous page, you will need to understand their causes.

Flexing This can be due to a number of factors. Insufficient support in the design. Hull material not substantial for the strains imposed. Fittings creating stress by having incorrect fastenings or support. Bad design or wrong supports on trolley or trailer. To help combat flexing, fit extra supports such as additional floor battens, struts on centrecases, timber pads or extra layers of resin and tape.

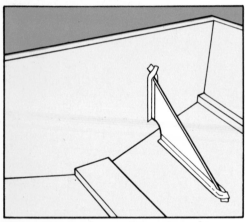

Strengthening knee using resin and tape.

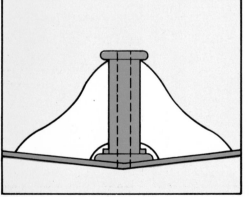

Stiffening the centrecase. Note runnels.

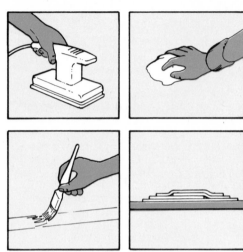

Strengthen GRP with resin and tape.

Hard Spots These can be caused by a part of the hull construction ending too abruptly, thus creating too much stress at a relatively small area. They can also occur when a bulkhead is fitted too tight so that it causes distortion. The stress cracks set up by this latter defect will follow the line of the bulkhead.

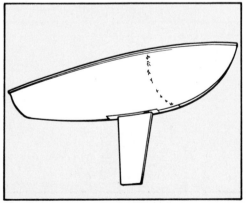

Hard spots around a bulkhead.

Impact Damage Minor damage caused by impact often goes unnoticed. A stone underneath a boat full of water will crack the hull skin or at the least break the surface coating. Shackles or blocks striking the same area of hull or deck over a period of time can cause substantial damage. If left unattended, these problems will spread.

Types of impact damage.

Ageing As a boat gets older, glues and resins used in its construction become brittle and lose their strength. Flexing of the hull and poor maintenance will hasten this process and cause broken joins and seams.

Weathering If coatings are allowed to flake off the surface, rot will set in. Weathering is caused by inadequate covers and accentuated by excessive wear and poor maintenance. Boats are not directly affected by frost or freezing. However, if wood or GRP become saturated with water which then freezes, delamination will occur.

Trapped Water Keep a lookout on all boats. On wood it will produce black stains. Drainage can be improved by altering the angle at which the boat is stored, or by creating or widening runnels. If a crack remains unnoticed on any boat, trapped water will saturate the surrounding surface area. Buoyancy tanks without adequate ventilation will darken wooden decks immediately above. Shrunken filler and redundant screwholes will also attract water.

Glue Joins must always be repaired before coating. Keep an eye on all glue joins on your boat. On wooden boats the most frequent joins to fail are the floor battens and rubbing beads. As indicated, check also centrecases, side seats and transoms. Replace parts if practical. Otherwise scrape out a 'V' and fill with epoxy filler. On GRP boats wooden pads can absorb moisture, swell and eventually break the bonding with the inert glassfibre material.

Stains caused by trapped water.

Osmosis This condition only occurs on GRP and is caused by air bubbles trapped in and under the gel coat resin during manufacture. It is more common on boats kept on moorings, when it occurs below the waterline. It can also be brought about by long periods of hot weather. An air bubble in the gel coat means that the coating is too thin, thus allowing water to permeate through the gel into a void. A strong solution forms in the bubble and builds up pressure in the void until it finally bursts through the outer skin. A chain reaction is caused with other bubbles until the water has a free passage direct to the laminate. Water will spread through the laminate by capillary action.

Wicking This condition is brought about during the laying up process when the chopped strand mat penetrates the gel coat, thus allowing direct access of water through the very thin or non-existent gel coat. Water then travels by capillary action through the mat, which will then distort the gel coat at a weak spot and create osmotic pressure, far from the point of water entry.

Wicking occurs during manufacture.

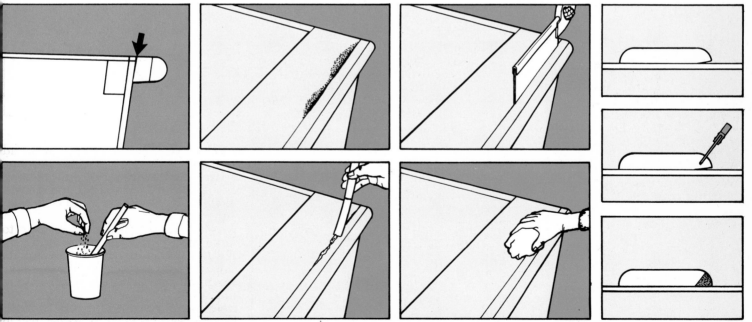

Failed glue joins bring about water damage. Watch rubbing beads and floor battens in particular. Build up with epoxy filler.

CENTRECASES

The centrecase is the focal point of any hull interior, and takes most of the stresses. If you understand the construction of your centrecase, you will be able to deal with any problems that occur.

Start by checking what method has been used to fit the case into the hull. On GRP it will either be moulded, or fixed as a separate unit using wooden bedlogs. On wood, the case will either be glued into position, or bedded on a mastic tape. The case structure is held by the thwart, which is either glued, screwed or nailed, just aft of the centre point. It should also have strong supports in the middle and at the front end of the case. Then check how the case is supported against sideways strain. On GRP there will be fibreglass moulding or aluminium tubing, while on wood there will be knees.

All centrecases have packing pieces fore and aft. These packing pieces determine the width of the slot and consequently the thickness of the centreboard. They are normally hardwood, and wide enough to join onto the sides of the case using a double row of fastenings. Dinghies which have a central spine use this as the core of the packing pieces, which locks the case into place. The bedlogs are the rails at the bottom edge of the case, which stiffen the sides of the case and fix the case to the hog. The top of the centrecase is supported by longitudinal rails, and has a capping to prevent the slot from distorting. Dagger board cases do not have cappings, but rely solely upon the rails.

The centrecase should be treated on the inside during assembly to prevent

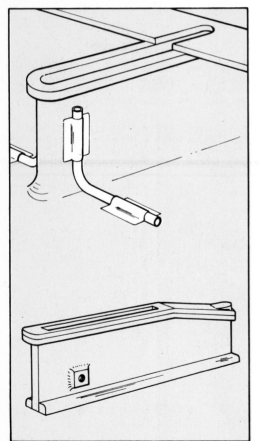

Methods of fitting case to GRP hull.

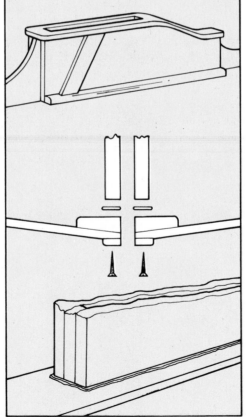

Methods of fitting case to wooden hull.

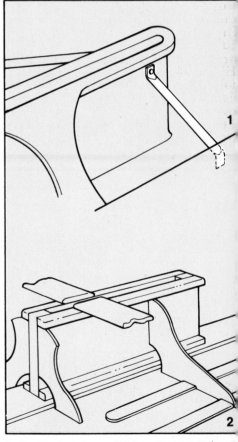

Sideways strain: 1. GRP and 2. wood boats

ot. This is done with applications of wood preserver, a paint which gives a smoother surface, or else with epoxy resin, the last coat of which contains graphite to reduce friction. Where Class Rules permit, you can glue plastic laminate to the inside faces of the case for easier movement. If repainting is necessary, turn the boat on its side and apply paint with a piece of carpet glued onto a stick.

The centreboard can be pivoted in two possible ways. You can either use a bolt fitted with rubber washers to prevent leaks through the bolt hole. Strengthen the bearing point for the bolt with a timber pad glued to the side of the case and extending down to the bedlogs. Take care not to bolt too tight and thus pinch the sides of the case. The other form of pivot is a stirrup fitting, which consists of two side straps and a sleeve bearing forming an 'H'. The sleeve is positioned in the pivot hole of the centreboard, the straps are clamped into the sleeve and the assembly complete with centreboard is then slid into the case slot. The straps are then screwed to either the top or the

bottom of the case. They should be sunk into the side of the case to reduce the gap between the case and the centreboard.

With moulded centrecases on GRP boats, check for flexing of the structure. This is shown by hinge cracking along the base of the case. Use resin and tape to strengthen the fillet. Do this on both sides to stop any leaks. Then check the supports, as these could be the cause of flexing.

If the centrecase is glued into the dinghy, check the glue join frequently. This join can break and cause leaks. Once it has broken, the only sure way of making a lasting repair is to remove the case and reglue. For a temporary repair, cover both sides of the join with resin and tape. However, water could still be trapped under the case itself.

If the centrecase is bedded on mastic tape, the join will last for four or five years. If leaks occur, the case can easily be removed and rebedded. Reseal the two surfaces of the join with resin or varnish before applying the mastic. After two weeks, tighten the screws holding the case.

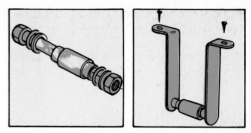

Pivots: bolt or stirrup fitting.

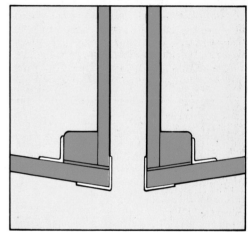

Tape both sides of the join.

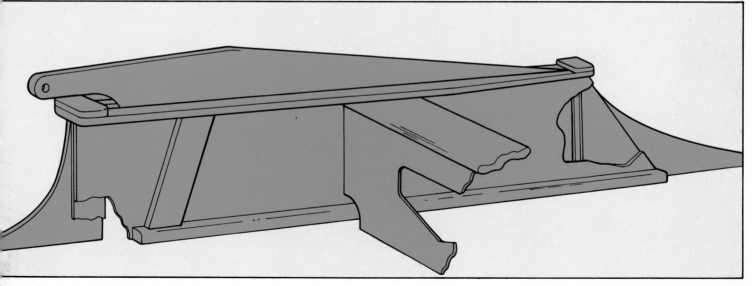

General construction of a centrecase.

INDEX